The Seven Woods
of Coole

The Seven Woods of Coole

A NOVEL BY

Franklin Lafayette King

*t*P
Texture Press
2013

The Seven Woods of Coole

Copyright © 2013 Franklin L. King
All rights reserved

Published in the United States by
Texture Press
1108 Westbrooke Terrace
Norman, OK 73072

For ordering information,
visit the Texture Press website at
www.texturepress.org.

ISBN-13: 978-0615816913
ISBN-10: 0615816916

Paintings by Franklin L. King
Photographs by Franklin L. King, Franklin L. King, IV,
and James Allison King
Poems, unless otherwise noted, are by the author

Book design by Arlene Ang

The Gathering

Spirits dwell upon the steps.

Orb of light appears within a wooded place.

Guests are silent yet song is played by wind-tossed branch.

The sound of tinkling glass within a stream.

Lovers walk in leaf-cast shade.

My voice speaks to that not present yet seen in shadow.

Lady Gregory, as I first knew her, was a plainly dressed woman of forty-five, without obvious good looks, except the charm that comes from strength, intelligence and kindness.

W. B. Yeats

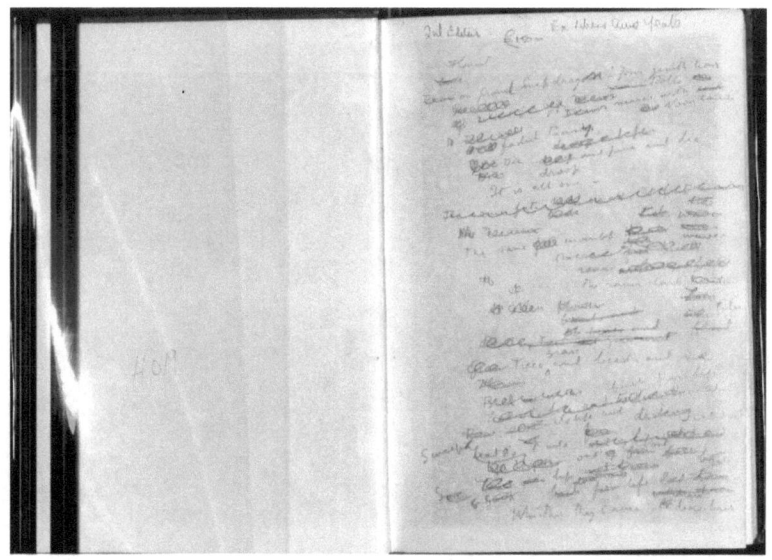

Handwritten notes inscribed upon the flyleaf of "The Shadowy Waters," 1902, Second Edition, purchased from the Anna Yeats Library.

Courtesy of the James Allison King collection.

Dedicated to
Christine, Frank, and James.

Introductory Lines to "The Shadowy Waters"

BY W. B. YEATS

To Lady Gregory

I walked among the seven woods of Coole:
Shan-walla, where a willow-bordered pond
Gathers the wild duck from the winter dawn;
Shady Kyle-dortha; sunnier Kyle-na-no,
Where many hundred squirrels are as happy
As though they had been hidden by green boughs
Where old age cannot find them; Paire-na-lee,
Where hazel and ash and privet blind the paths:
Dim Pairc-na-carraig, where the wild bees fling
Their sudden fragrances on the green air;
Dim Pairc-na-tarav, where enchanted eyes
Have seen immortal, mild, proud shadows walk;
Dim Inchy wood, that hides badger and fox
And marten-cat, and borders that old wood
Wise Buddy Early called the wicked wood:
Seven odours, seven murmurs, seven woods.

Table of Contents

❧1❧
The Reception

"A fine party it is tonight, Professor and such an honor, too. You deserve more recognition than the University has bestowed upon you. Anyone that writes a definitive work in any subject area deserves respect, but when you take on W.B. Yeats, you deserve adoration, if not jealousy, from your fellow scholars," said Department Chair Fuller as he avoided eye contact with the noted scholar.

The Professor of Literature felt ill at ease. He was most at home at his estate house, Mt. Gilead; that large five-bay house from another era with its rows of dark, unlit windows and loose stone façade that had denied the entrance of nature for centuries. Even the water dripping from the roof evoked a peaceful metronome feeling within him.

While a handsome, youthful man, he had not pursued his fellow female academicians. "Always time for that, always time," he would mutter to himself. His outer appearance cloaked the aged scholar within. He had no desire to entertain guests at Mt. Gilead. The dark wood walls of his study were consolation enough for him. Odors within the house were typical of the large, landed estate houses of pastoral Ireland. The musty smell of leather-bound books mixed with the scent of cigar and brandy, yet with a hint of mint to provide freshness to the house.

"Here, Professor, I have brought you another pint of Guinness. I know that you are the kind that enjoys a good drink."

"What kind is that?" the Professor responded with mild agitation.

"Oh, I am sorry, sir. I meant no disrespect to you. I mean that you seem to have a great appreciation for all things of quality whether they are a beautiful woman or a fine drink of Irish brew."

With that comment, the Professor accepted the pint and sipped heartily from it. He loved the taste of Guinness and the smell of cigars. Every Anglo-Irish gentleman must occasionally forgo the more acceptable drinks of the upper class to revisit his more humble roots. "It has something to do with an Irishman's love of the earth," his mother would say never quite explaining her meaning.

The Professor began to feel somewhat loose about the feet after so many toasts. He was more comfortable with old shoes, rum-soaked cigars and simmering tea. "What do they know about how I feel about my work?

Soulless to say the least; I only copy greatness, not create it," he said silently to himself.

"Professor, you must speak at the faculty senate again. We cannot get enough of you these days," Dr. Beatrice Murphy said with sparkling eyes and raised glass.

"Beatrice Murphy, what does she know of writing?" he thought. "Spinster with narrow-beaded stare always searching for that which cannot be found; committed feminist yet stalker of men."

Fellow Professor John Camp approached the Professor. "A good party on your behalf; nice to see that the University has funding for such an event."

"John, I am glad you could attend. I really did not expect you to take the time."

"Would not have missed it, old friend. Since you are an international expert on Mr. Yeats, I do have a couple of questions to ask," he said while munching on a cheese straw. Small fragments fell to the pine floor or got captured within his beard.

"John, you have never hesitated to ask a question. I would not expect you to be meek now; so fire away."

"I have often wondered about so brilliant a mind as that of Mr. Yeats believing in the afterlife. I guess that is what you would call it."

"There are many names for it," responded the Professor.

"Well, anyway, I remember reading, since you revived him for us, that he believed in séances and other such nonsense."

"Yes, he was a different type of person. As you may recall, séances and Ouija boards were very much in vogue during his lifetime especially during the late Victorian period. I think that for many, however, they were merely party games rather than sincere beliefs in the occult or afterlife."

"So you are rationalizing that he was just being trendy," Professor Camp added with a smile and a wink to others that were standing nearby.

"I must admit that he was probably more involved in it than most. After all, we all seek to know what exists beyond this life."

"There is a difference between research and longing, don't you agree, Professor?" Dr. Camp remarked.

"So it seems since you have made a good living with your patents based upon animal models. I have often wondered do your radical approaches to deviant behavior work on humans as well?" asked the Professor.

Dr. Camp's eyes narrowed as he sipped his dark red wine. "I understand that W.B. was a member of several secret societies: I guess that is what you would call them. As a published and well respected professor of psychology, such deviant behavior has always fascinated me."

"The gift of genius is often looked at as deviant."

Dr. Camp continued, "I understand that he underwent the Portal Ritual for entry in the Inner Order of the Golden Dawn as well as being a proponent, perhaps even the founder, of the Celtic Mystical Order."

"Yes, that is correct. You appear to have prepared yourself for our discussion," responded the Professor.

"He even fell for a psychic machine that could receive messages from the other side. Then on top of it all, he married Georgia Hyde Lees who believed in automatic writing. Now let's see if I can get this right, it involves writing that is done at the subconscious level; something to do with spirits taking control of one's hand," Dr. Camp said as he smiled sarcastically.

He then added, "George was a unique case, in my opinion, of trying to hold onto W.B. at a time that he was sexually active with other women. In other words, she could not compete with the other gals in looks, but she could join him in his intellectual pursuit of the spirit world."

Again Dr. Camp looked around for an audience. "I am surprised that he is not communicating with someone like you, Professor, from his current residency in the graveyard of St. Columba's at Duncliff." Several faculty members, who had come nearer to enjoy the sport of professional rivalry, laughed at the comment.

"Dr. Camp, I would prefer not to discuss this side of Mr. Yeats' character at this time."

"If not now, when may I ask?" queried Dr. Camp.

"I suggest that you find something sharp to sit upon until there is a more appropriate time and place for our discussion." This time the audience of eavesdroppers laughed even louder.

The Professor noticed a gentleman with sandy hair standing quietly near the wall on the opposite side of the throng of well-wishers and inquisitors. He was wearing a well-worn tweed jacket and mismatched pants. To the Professor he appeared to be an academician or perhaps an unemployed barrister. The Professor noticed that he was carrying a rather large portfolio case in his hands; the dark leather style popular in the 19th century.

After more discussions with friends and those that claimed to be, the Professor poured himself another drink. The unknown gentleman then approached him. "Sir, you probably do not remember me, but when you taught the introductory Irish Literary Movement class for the first time at Trinity, I was one of your students. I was the timid freckle-faced lad that sat at the back of your class and never said a word. I must admit I was very afraid of you at the time."

"I somewhat recall a young intense fellow that never looked up from his books and notes. I trust that you are not still upset at the grade that I gave you."

"I am sure that was me. My name is Sean McAllister. By the way, you gave me an A."

"Well Sean, I am honored you took the time to stop by."

"I could not help but offer you my own personal congratulations. In addition, I wanted to give you this," he said as he extended the portfolio case to the Professor.

"What is it?" asked the Professor.

"It is a gift to you. Your course altered my life in that I later became a professor of Irish literature at an American university." Sean paused. "If you have a moment, I would like to tell you about the contents of the case."

"Please go ahead," replied the Professor.

"You had been lecturing about Lady Gregory and her relationship to W.B. Yeats when you mentioned her home, Coole Park near Gort. Later, I mentioned your lecture to my mother who, at that time, did not feel that she had invested wisely in her son's academic career."

The Professor replied, "It was truly a lovely place. I spent many enjoyable hours walking through the park. Thank goodness they preserved the fine trees, wild meadows and turloughs of the estate. I wish that they could have done the same for Coole House. It is comforting to know, or at least I believe so, that the park meant more to her than did the house."

Sean continued, "I too have walked through the seven woods of Coole Park. They are indeed lovely and worthy of preservation. My time spent there in my youth proved to be an oasis for my soul.

"Professor, my father was a member of the demolition team hired by the Irish government in 1941 to destroy the house after Lady Gregory's death. I feel that when she deeded the property over to the State, she never intended for her home at Coole Park to be destroyed. The only things of significant remaining today are the steps, garden walls and the autograph tree. I read some old clippings where a government official claimed that it was wartime, and that there was not sufficient funding to restore the house properly. He also stated in the clipping that her memory would be best preserved without the structure; pure rationalization I believe."

"Yes, that was truly a great loss to the Irish people. So many memories and even legends are associated with that house and the park itself. The grounds alone contain unique naturalist treasures in the form of the variety of trees, grasses, and I might add, its unique turloughs; those vanishing bodies of water."

"Yes, sir, that is why I am here. My father found a collection of what he called, 'insignificant art' hidden within a paneled wall of her library. Even though I am sure there was a release latch, it was only after the wrecking crew had split through the paneling that the paintings were found. One crewmember threw it upon the pile of debris to be burned but my father grabbed it back. He thought he might be able to fetch a coin or two for it.

"Even though he thought the gift had little significant value, other than a shilling or two, he took it home to my mother," Sean continued. "My Mum said that she, being a proper Catholic mother, did not want that kind of trash hanging on anyone's wall. She then took the paintings and put them in the waste can outside our tenement building before my father tried to sell them.

"Since she made such an unpleasant uproar about it, I, being an early adolescent, took the art and hid it in my bedroom trunk. There it was to remain all these years even after I moved to America. My wife, a professor also of Irish Literature, was throwing things away recently when she discovered the paintings. I had, myself, forgotten that they even existed. Since she had read about your recognition, she suggested I give the art to you."

The professor began to look at the scrolled canvases within the case. He first noticed a piece of faded, yellow paper frayed on its edges. When opened, it read: "My Beloved."

Sean continued as the Professor held the paper and assortment of canvases in his hands, "Even though the paintings are not signed on the front, on the back of one painting is the word 'William' and the date 1896; both of which were written in pencil.

"Professor, at first my father was thrilled, thinking he had discovered some paintings of Jack Yeats. He never assumed that William Butler Yeats, the brother of Jack Yeats, might have wanted to paint himself. However, realizing how limited his talents were with brush, he later decided to write instead. In an age before portable photography, as we know it today existed, the best way to retain a memory was to paint it.

"Something unusual also occurred that I must relate to you. My father said the portfolio was wrapped in a love knot of ivy. He tore the brittle, dried vine from the portfolio thinking that ivy had earlier penetrated the wall and then died from lack of sunlight. Finding the paintings to appear new, he dismissed them believing that they were of very recent origin; their colors bright and intense. He thought for a moment he heard the sounds of a forest bird, perhaps that of a raven. Professor, I don't know what it means. My father loved a good story and perhaps he just created one to amuse both my mother and myself. We were very poor and desperate for the *craic* regardless of what form it took."

"Thank you Shawn, even though it appears that an untalented person must have drawn these primitive works of art, perhaps even Lady Gregory's son at an early age, I will cherish them as a gift from you and your wife."

The professor placed the portfolio case near to his topcoat so that he would remember to take it home.

❧2❧
Mt. Gilead

The Professor left the University Club party early for snowflakes were beginning to fall along the coast of Connemara; small flakes blowing like the ashes from a great fire upon Ben Bulben. He knew that he was too filled with Jameson and Guinness to drive safely that night. Yet he cranked his VW sedan and drove to the unattended gates of the University; the wheels of his small car spinning when patches of ice were encountered. He struggled to fasten his seatbelt, "No need to be embraced by a strap this night. If I am sober enough to crank the car, then I am sober enough to drive it." He laughed to himself.

The road to Mt. Gilead House was winding and very narrow. The Professor had to lean close to the windshield to see through the falling snow. Suddenly, a small deer crossed in front of him. He swerved to miss the fleeing animal. "What! Lady Evans can't even keep her domestic deer locked up much less her drunken philandering husband. If he had been on the lane, she would have paid me not to swerve," he said as he encountered another patch of ice. The small car suddenly left the narrow road, hit a hedgerow, slowed, and then slammed the front fender into the concealed stone wall of a field.

The Professor, amid his profanities, fell forward striking his head upon the windshield after also receiving a great deal of the impact upon his chest.

He did not remember how long he sat motionless in the still running automobile; the window now completely covered by fresh snow. Even though the pain in his chest and head were intense, he put the car into reverse and reentered the road only to find that it was very difficult to steer. "Thank goodness, I am now within walking distance of Mt. Gilead, my oldest and best friend." He parked the car, still in the road, and walked slowly towards the house.

Soon he staggered to the steps and managed to stabilize himself on the stone banisters that led to the double doors. Upon entering the house, he felt its cold breath and the impression of its intense indifference to his condition. The house had a scent of mint about it. The Professor always kept dried leaves in vases in order to give the rooms a cleaner odor. In summer, the rooms smelt of fresh mint which, with what few guests he had, yielded a most delightful aroma.

As he entered the parlor, he placed the paintings on a table. There he sat for several minutes staring at the tightly scrolled collection. "What nonsense! At best, primitive paintings by an unknown relative or even a child. They were not even worth the cost of a frame."

The Professor placed four kerosene moistened logs within the hearth and struck a match upon the intricately carved 16th century marble mantelpiece leaving a black streak upon its face like many others before him had done.

Even though disoriented from both drink and the impact of the collision, the Professor intended to read the first two chapters of his favorite student's dissertation on the Irish Literary Revival. The "introduction" and "review of the literature" were to him the least dry of the many required epistles to be read. He was also very pleased when a student referenced one of his many works in an attempt to expand the realm of academic knowledge or to gain favor with the Professor.

The Irish Literary Revival had interested him since he was a freshman at the University of Galway. He was fascinated by the writings of John Millington Synge, Sean O'Casey, George Bernard Shaw, Edward Martyn, William Butler Yeats and Lady Augusta Gregory. Why, he wondered, would these people create such strong bonds in the highly competitive world of the literary arts? He knew the jealousy between highly creative individuals was extreme. He understood the unwritten rule that a writer, even an academic one, should never ask another author to critique his work any more than an artist should ask another to provide an honest appraisal of his paintings.

He would not admit it to his students, but the lives of the literary masters appealed to him more than did their publications. Their literary contributions were work to him; words to be dissected; word counts, connotations, textual meanings, rhythm and flow. Their lives, however, were pure pleasure to him. As he read their contributions, he inwardly wore the mask of the truly gifted.

The undocumented time between their writings was the most fascinating of all to him, but this was not to be admitted to his students. "Pure speculation," he would comment when a student would ask a question whose answer was not clearly written on a well-researched page. As a professor, he demanded that his students be accountable for every statement written in their scholarly pursuit. "Never too many citations," he would mumble when thumbing through a student's work.

What had most intrigued him privately was the relationship between Lady Augusta Gregory and W. B. Yeats. While admittedly, they both loved poetry and a wide variety of dramatic works, his admiration for her, however, had gone well beyond scholarly attraction. He knew that Yeats had dedicated many of his writings to Augusta as well as his having frequently mentioned her in his letters to Georgiana. Yeats' castle was near Coole Park House making him a frequent and opportunistic visitor to Lady Gregory. Coole Park, that large and beautiful estate house, commanded both respect and envy by its sheer size alone.

Coole House had been acquired by Lady Gregory's husband, Sir William Henry Gregory, a man of intellect and privileged birth. He, however, was addicted to horse racing which had an adverse impact on the financial bearing of the family. While not an accomplished writer, he did possess an interest in the arts and classical languages. Had their ages been more similar, their relationship might have taken a more enduring course.

Isabella Augusta Persse married Sir Gregory on March 4, 1880. She was then his second wife. Sir Gregory was 35 years older than Ms. Persse. In an age when wealth and position were valued above all else, their marriage was very much accepted by society. He had wed a beautiful young intellect, and she had obtained a title as well as the wealth that properly belonged to the Anglo-Irish aristocracy of Ireland. To the proper Victorian lady, the desires of the flesh were of little value and even less discussed. Yet Augusta was not to be stereotyped by the demands of society nor was she to be fitted to one single role; that of a beautiful woman on the arm of an elderly gentleman.

Having read two chapters from the dissertation on "W. B. Yeats and His Relationship to Nature," the Professor bent his head low upon his chest; the cigar but ash and the black tea cold. Small crumbs of soda bread remained upon the desktop as well. His scholar's mind was thick like molasses, the heavy tones of chimes having sounded the hour when all but the owl slept under a fog shrouded moon.

Late it was that night. Only the wind moved the leafless limbs of the winter tree. The moon soon left the ridge of the frost-covered mountain to seek the warmth of a tropic sun. 'Bold,' 'afraid': frail words to describe the night when spirits moved about the grounds of Mt. Gilead seeking entry within.

The fire sounded a loud snap as sparks fled the play of smoke and burning logs. The snapping logs aroused the Professor from his sleep; he sat upright immediately. The smoke of the hearth turned to steam as the professor gazed in amazement. A large coal-burning engine was seen slowly entering the Kingsbridge Station. The smartly styled clothing worn by those in attendance was that of the early 1930s as gentlemen and ladies in hats stood by to board their respective trains.

The conductor in Dublin's Kingsbridge Station noticed a tall, older gentleman pacing back and forth on the platform. Occasionally, the future passenger would look at his large, gold pocket watch suspended upon a similarly made chain; his wool suit well-worn about the elbows and cuffs. "Rumpled," the conductor thought as though the man had spent a forth night in it. He didn't like unkempt men riding in his cars.

The passenger appeared to be in his late 60s or early 70s. The conductor kept trying to remember where he had seen him before. He realized that he knew this man somehow but could not recall the "what and where" of him. Then he remembered. "The Abbey Theater. That's it. I saw him there years ago with Lady Augusta Gregory or at least my friend said that was her with the black dress and cold expression; almost birdlike she was. That must be him, the great playwright and poet. Well, I'll be; the saints have blessed me this day. I will have to tell the wife who I saw today at the station."

William entered the car and sat down at the shared tabletop of two opposing seats. Outside, the rain was beginning to fall upon the open station as passengers fled to find their cars and the conductor sounded the departure. He was in no mood to talk to anyone; not this day. His brown travel trunk he had placed on the seat opposite him to keep anyone else from occupying it.

In his hand was a telegram that he kept opening and then wadding up, only to open and read it again. Then he left it opened on the tabletop and wrote repeatedly the day's date, 23 May 1932. The context of the note was very simple and to the point: "Lady Augusta Gregory. Near death. Asking for you. Come immediately. Coole Park, Mary Shannon, Maid."

Lady Gregory's driver picked William up in Galway for the drive to Gort; they sat silently in the limousine as it sped past beneath the overhanging limbs of the seven woods of Coole.

The Professor then saw a man running to the steps of Coole Park. He flung one of the great doors open and entered the dark quiet entry hall. Then skipping steps he raced to Lady Gregory's bedroom. There before him lay the only person he had truly loved. Her aged body now covered with a white linen shroud. The silence of the room amazed him; a room that had known their love while wild birds sang within the woods of Coole.

The maid not knowing what to do had called both the Lady's physician and her own priest. Mary, never having learned to write, had asked the priest to prepare the telegram William had read on the train.

"Leave us, leave us! For the sake of all that is holy, leave us now!" William shouted.

The priest and doctor, upon their departure from the room, closed the door. William could hear their muffled conversation continuing down the wide ornate hall filled with the memorabilia of Sir Gregory's travels.

"Mary, you too must leave us now," he said quietly. "I need to talk to Augusta."

Mary seemed to understand and curtseyed in the fashion of the past as she left the room.

William knelt as a subject before her bed. At first he could utter no words. His tears moistened the linen shroud as he held her marble-like hand. "To have lain as one within the fairy ring! What have I done! What have I done!"

The Professor's hearth smoke turned to fog and then to a clear sky filled with warmth and billowing summer clouds. The Professor now saw a young man walking towards a large mansion. The woods are filled with the songs of birds and swans swimming in the lakes of Coole Park.

Beyond him is a large estate house of white stone; it walls painted thick with ivy that clings tenaciously to the structure. Its gray slate roof shows brightly in the colors of day. The Professor had only seen a painting of Coole House in the National Library of Ireland. Now he sees it clearly embraced by the sun and senses the myriad odors of the garden and the sweet smell of the wild fields beyond. The young man's sports coat and trousers captured sunlight in their weave, his black hair gathering sunlight like a reflection from the surface of a holy well.

William had been invited to the house to meet a middle-aged woman of 45. He somewhat dreaded the occasion since he expected it to be quiet dull; everyone sitting stiffly in hard chairs sipping tea too cool to be enjoyed; her examining every word for correct pronunciation and meaning.

What he did know of her, however, spoke of a highly intelligent and demanding woman. Some had described Lady Gregory as too proper and very cold to strangers that she deemed inferior to herself. Of course, these were just rumors. Perhaps he would discover her company to be pleasant; the afternoon tea an enjoyable experience.

He announced his arrival by the pulling of the bell cord.

❧ 3 ❧
Betrayal in Egypt

The morning of William and Edward Martyn's first visit to Coole Park, Augusta sat alone in the large study of her home. Sir Gregory had been dead for several years. His trophies and weaponry were well displayed in heavy oak cases. The windows were closed not yet allowing the fragrance of the garden to enter. Her feet were placed upon a thick Persian rug that rested upon the floor; above the mantelpiece hung an oil painting of the Nile.

She appeared to be a small person while seated in the large leather chair of her husband's. Her intellect far exceeded the dimensions of her body. She was adorned in a black satin dress with a high collar. Around her neck was a most unique necklace. It looked similar to a knight's medallion, its surface covered by beautiful white diamonds while the center stone was a radiant blue diamond of at least a caret in size.

Even though it was June 1894, Lady Gregory had a shawl about her shoulders. A small peat fire added but insignificant warmth to the large room. There was never a sense in Ireland that the weather was ever warm enough.

Augusta sipped her tea and closed her eyes. Before the arrival of her guests, her thoughts had taken her to Egypt and to her visit there with Sir Gregory. Her husband loved the arts and travel. His large and jovial frame concealed the fact that he was an accomplished Anglo-Irish writer, politician and sportsman. In 1871, he had been appointed Governor of Ceylon prior to his marriage to Augusta.

It was on her trip to Egypt in 1881 that she met the handsome and adventurous Wilfrid Scawen Blunt. Wilfrid was similar to Sir Gregory in that he was also a gifted writer in addition to being an accomplished poet. He, too was a traveler having visited Spain, Algeria, and the Syrian Desert in addition to the Middle East and India. It was Egypt; however, that he loved the most. Even though English, he was a supporter of the Irish cause of liberation from England. He had married well in 1869 giving him a prominent place in English society.

Sir Gregory was interested in horses since horse racing and losing his money were both passions of his. He knew Wilfrid kept fine Arabian horses on his landed estate in Egypt. As a courtesy to her husband, Augusta accompanied Sir Gregory during his discussions with the poet and lover of horses. Wilfrid's estate, Sheykh Obeyd, was more in keeping with British houses in the warm tropical areas of the British Empire. The house grounds consisted of 37 acres hidden behind walls of clay. Pomegranates, roses, vines and wondering exotic animals demanded the ongoing attention of a staff of 16 full-time caretakers. The pink clay house with three arches was surrounded by broad verandas that allowed for the free access of the winds that blew across the hot sands of Egypt. Its proximity to the Nile permitted the wind to carry the myriad scents of the gardens throughout the dwelling. Servants in white dress coats waited on every need of those who arrived.

"Wilfrid, I would like for you to meet my wife, Lady Augusta Gregory of Coole Park."

Wilfrid looked at Sir Gregory while raising his Waterford Crystal wine glass in a toast. "Sir, you have indeed found a young and most charming companion. I must congratulate you on your taste in both women and horses."

"Wilfrid, my man, I can assure you this, Augusta is not only charming but brilliant as well. She, like you, is a writer." Augusta remained silent as the two men described her attributes as though she too were to be auctioned like one of Wilfrid's prize stallions.

Sir Gregory continued, "Not only is she beautiful, but she has a keen appreciation of writing. In fact her plays and poetry have caused quite a stir in Irish society. I often have to scold her into remembering her place in society," he said while looking at Augusta, accompanied by both a smile and a most tender wink.

Wilfrid looked more closely at Augusta. "Madam, your husband has certainly praised you beyond the most obvious of your attributes. I see that we share a common interest. I look forward to our future discussions as I do with your husband, and I seek to find only the most suitable horses in my stables for your estate in Ireland."

Even though dressed in light linen of the most sophisticated weave, she softly blotted the perspiration that had formed about her lips and on her forehead. She could not help but observed the piercing stare of Wilfrid as he spoke to her.

Even though warm, he was properly dressed in the attire of an Englishman riding across the moors of Scotland. As he spoke, he held a leather riding whip in his hand; using it as a scribe to punctuate his words. Augusta could almost visualize the mystery behind his startlingly blue eyes that contrasted with the blackness of his hair; hair that her fingers were later to weave into a love knot the night before she and Sir Gregory departed for England and Ireland.

When the hour of tedious and polite discussion regarding the breeding of Arabian horses ended, the parties retired for the evening, each to separate bedrooms. Lady Gregory and Sir William had not slept in the same room since their marriage night. Being a large, older man, he had kept Augusta awake much of their wedding night with his heavy breathing.

In her chamber, she dressed in a white Egyptian cotton gown and began to read a volume of popular Victorian literature that had been placed most decoratively within the room by the servants; pages filled with restrained romance set in exotic lands. "What land was more romantic or dreamy than Egypt?" she thought.

Augusta had found Wilfrid to be a delightful flirt. While talking to Sir Gregory, he managed frequent eye contact with her. There was no doubt they shared much in common. Both of them felt that British rule was unfair to the indigenous populations: he for the peoples of Egypt and she for Ireland. Their mutual love of poets and poetry was also a common uniting factor. Yet it was the flirtations that interested her most. He had already acquired a reputation as a professional philanderer. She would later call him 'Lord Wilfrid' in that his similarities to Byron were striking.

The heat was heavy in the room; smells from the garden most pungent. She undid the top buttons of her chemise to allow more air to flow through her garment. Even that proved insufficient in the hot humid night.

She arose and walked out onto the moonlit veranda. Small beads of perspiration ran down between her breasts.

"Lady Gregory." The voice came from the darkened corner of the veranda; the image of a man appeared accented by the glow of his cigar. Instantly her heart raced in surprise at the deep voice with a perfect English accent.

"Wilfrid, you startled me. I did not expect to find anyone awake at this hour of the night. The house is so quiet; I had assumed that all, including the staff, had gone to sleep. The heat is so dreadful even with the paddle fan. I think it must be the humidity. What am I saying; a desert should be very dry?"

"Your first assumption was correct," Wilfrid responded. "The Nile often floods causing water to sit in the fields. That in itself is enough to make this a very humid night."

"I thought that the moon was to be my only companion. With it, a poet appears," she said, her smile concealed in the dim light of the moon.

"My Lady, you do have special powers. Even both the moon and I obey your wishes." With those words, Wilfrid drew near to her placing his hand upon the porch railing. They stood so close yet not touching. Both Augusta and Wilfrid could feel the energy and dynamic presence of the other; an aura that surpassed her understanding; a feeling not shared with Sir Gregory.

Small clouds from the Mediterranean moved across the face of the full moon. "The clouds are wiping the tears from the face of the moon," said Augusta. The heavy smells of Egypt were in the air; odors of blooming pomegranates, red honeysuckle, date palms and the reed-filled banks of the Nile emitted their own unique scents.

❧4❧
The Visitor

From her library at Coole Park, Lady Gregory had a view of the lawns in front of her opulent house. The open fields, interspersed with aged beech and oak trees, were covered in blooming wild flowers. Snap dragons could be seen among meadows of wild orchids and maidenhair. Summer clouds moved by sea winds traveled across the land from off the Connemara Coast; that beautiful land of rough seas, towering cliffs and steep granite mountains.

The large Irish wolfhound at her feet also sensed someone, yet unseen, approaching. The only sounds heard in the house were the ticking of the hall clock and the occasional snap of burning log.

On the bridge that crossed the small flowing stream were two young men. They were obviously good friends since the taller one kept placing his arm around the shoulder of the other. Occasionally, they appeared to be laughing; striking one another's shoulders in a playful mood. How different they were from her aged husband; so full of life and joviality. Edward's smile could be seen at a great distance.

She had expected to have tea with Edward Martyn and his unknown friend. Who was the taller man who appeared to be in command? His black hair, erect posture adding a very distinctive manner about him; his glasses did not detract from his appearance but added a mature, scholarly appeal.

Edward Martyn was a playwright, a cultural activist and a political figure; each attribute had attracted her to him. While not a handsome man, his jovial nature made him a delight to know, and she very much enjoyed their conversations that often lasted into the evenings. He was much in demand for his musical talents being one of Ireland's finest organists. His knowledge of the great composers and his lively discussions, related to the language of music, were always guaranteed to entertain. If a great house did not possess an organ, then a piano would certainly do for an evening's entertainment. Edward had found himself too busy for marriage; matrimony, an idea that his family strongly supported if the traditions of the household and its bloodline were to continue.

She then remembered that Edward had earlier mentioned to her that someday he would like to bring a guest for the afternoon; a young aspiring poet and playwright. He had assured her there could be, but little doubt, that a bond would later be formed between each of them.

Upon entering the library, Lady Gregory was impressed by the commanding presence of William. She extended her hand to him which he lightly kissed. He then stepped back performing a slight bow of recognition to her position and title. "How straight and tall he stands," she thought. She could not help but feel a slight attraction to this stranger.

William looked about the large room with its fine woodwork and plaster ceiling. He noticed the slight rounding of the ceiling; typical of the great Irish estates houses. Outside, the garden and meadow birds could be heard, rejuvenated by the warmth of the sun and the brilliant hue of the sky.

William looked directly into her eyes. "Lady Gregory, you have a most beautiful home amongst the flowers and turloughs of Coole Park. While passing one of the smaller lakes, I could not help but notice the beautiful white swans gliding upon the surface. The reflection of the wood and the quietness of the water made the swans and ducks appear like images painted in nature's most beautiful composition."

"Thank you for recognizing the wild and ever changing beauty that I can never hope to own. My husband chose this estate most wisely. I am very pleased he did not choose to reside permanently in London or Dublin. Only in nature can we observe the works of the god or gods that we believe in. I can only hope the composition you referred to can remain untouched."

"Lady Gregory," commented Edward, "you must take credit yourself for much of the natural beauty that Mr. Yeats has seen today. You see, William, her ladyship has been busy altering nature. Some would say, improving upon it."

"Edward, you do not need to be so honest with our guest so soon. You take the awe and mystery of what he has seen and explain it as a botanist might. As a poet, he must not be interested in the process but in the results that inspire him. Is it not the collective that exceeds the whole?"

"Mr. Yeats, what color are your eyes? Blue like the sky above us or dark brown like the autumn leaves that soon will fall about us?"

At her words, William removed his glasses and moved closer to Lady Gregory. He did not know how to feel about her question. "What was the intention of it?" he wondered. "What relevancy is there in the color of a man's eyes or is it her desire to observe me more closely?" He then remembered: *the eye is the passageway to the soul.*

"Edward, I see you have once again been involved in politics. My advice to you is to be careful. The Irish nationalist often cannot tell friend from foe. Assassination is not an impossibility in our land of conflict. We all desire the same thing, but we express it so differently. What do you think, Mr. Yeats?"

"Lady Gregory, I feel that the most important way to communicate our emotions is through verse. Let the reader interpret the meaning of the rhyme. Some will say that we are for this, and others will say just the opposite. In a time of turmoil, truth is voiceless; emotion is the ruler of thoughts."

"Mr. Yeats, I believe that you are speaking in riddles just to confuse us. A man of your assumed brilliance should speak clearly."

"Lady Gregory, I am like the surface of your lake, the wind determines the direction of the ripples not the lake itself or even the one that owns it. The wind is not seen yet present."

"Mr. Yeats, I will need to be careful of you. Perhaps your actions will speak more clearly to us than your words have this day. I can only assume that you are for the liberation of Ireland from those that oppress the common people."

"Lady Gregory, I am a champion of freedom in an idyllic world." As he spoke, he noticed the intensity of her eyes and the firmness of her lips. Humor had fled from the discussion.

Suddenly beside Lady Gregory was a young lad of 15. It was as though he had appeared far too suddenly to be real. "William, I want you to meet my son, Robert. Edward and he are already best friends." Both men extended their hands. Robert dutifully shook them, bowing his head politely to each visitor.

"Robert has only two interests: becoming a great artist and sailing with wings upon the wind. I think he has read too much fiction, but he insists he will fly one day just like the birds of Coole Park. I just hope he is a more graceful flyer than our swans.

In Robert's hand was a sketch of wild birds. "Well Augusta, I think that he has already obtained one of his dreams; that of becoming an artist," commented Edward.

"Edward, please don't feed his ambitions or his ego. I am afraid that his destiny will soon be out of my hands."

"Mr. Yeats, a poet and a playwright. Since you are so silent, except when questioned, I must ask if you are a revolutionary as well?"

"Lady Gregory, I think that being a poet and playwright is ambitious enough. I have yet to be accomplished at either; at least I am told by my all too many critics that accuse me of being more a follower of Shelley than an original composer of rhythmic thought."

"First, William, you must call me 'Augusta.' It is true that I have not read of you, but you do seem to have an honest grip on thoughts. I am certain that both Ireland and I will hear more of you in the future. Now, however, I am not so certain of your jovial friend," she said as she smiled at Edward.

Augusta glanced once more towards the tall stranger. "William, you have chosen your friend wisely. Not only is he creative, he is wealthy as well. I am hoping to talk him into helping me form an Irish Literary Theatre. I think that I have his interest, since I promised him that if he provides the funding, then his plays will be performed not just in his thoughts, as they are now, but on a lighted stage. Vanity should be used wisely as I have just demonstrated on your friend." Augusta laughed. "By the way, where are you staying while you are visiting Edward?"

"Augusta, I am staying with him at Tulira Castle."

"My, Edward, you are a show off." Tulira Castle, built in the 15th century, was indeed a grand house. The castle itself had been built by McHubert Burke and later acquired by the Martyn family. The mansion added to by the Martyn family has consumed the much earlier castle. Even Coole Park, with all of its grandeur and extensive parks, cannot be compared to Tulira. It was a home meant to impress all that see it. The house, by itself, was an architectural expression; an exclamation point of design.

Edward replied, "My home, being not far from your estate here at Gort, is but a challenging walk for William. I failed to add one thing he was too modest to mention. Even though his brother Jack is an accomplished artist, Mr. Yeats enjoys the canvas as well. Not that he has any talent mind you." Edward smiled at William who failed to find the humor in his remark.

Lady Gregory glanced towards the young man. "William, you must promise to return to Coole Park and paint. The season is warm, and the gardens are filled with blooms. I hope that you, in return for my tea and conversation this afternoon, will render in oil both my house and the flowers within my garden. If you do so, I will reward you by placing your art work on the paneled wall over there." She pointed to one of the few unadorned portions of her library wall. "Whatever you paint will be in a position to capture the fleeting afternoon light without fading the colors of your canvas."

"Augusta, you flatter me in assuming that I have even the most rudimental talent. Edward sees me more objectively. Later if you deem my work worthy, I would love to paint a portrait of you." William spoke with a boldness he did not recognize within himself.

"No, no, you should seek out subjects that a young man's heart fancy more. As you can clearly see, I have not the glorious coloring of the true Irish or of the orchids within the garden. My pale English skin does not deserve to be painted. In addition, I lack the fullness of lips that appeal to the Irish taste. I want my memory to be contained only in the written word or in the literary gifts I give to others."

William responded, "You fault me too severely, Madam. I am not interested in what others consider to be beauty. Let me be the judge of what beauty is. I insist that you allow me to capture you upon canvas. I noticed that there is a willow-bordered pond at Shan-walla that would be a perfect place for me to paint you. That is what I believe Edward called that particular wooded area of your estate."

"Yes, Shan-walla is one of the seven woods of Coole," she said in amazement to his insistence.

"I will be staying only a few days with Edward before my return to Sligo. Would you be willing to sit for me tomorrow, say two-ish?"

"You do make assumptions. Am I to trust your virtue or are you to trust mine?" She laughed.

William did not know what to think of such a bold statement from a woman of such aristocratic birth and intelligence. Both her directness and honesty challenged him.

Augusta laughed. "I did not mean to give you so much to ponder upon our first meeting together. I will have one of my house staff serve us while you paint. Mary will ensure your safety as well as my reputation."

"Then it is settled, you will sit for me?" William asked.

"Yes, despite my better judgment," she said with a smile.

❧ 5 ❧
Tulira Castle

In the gray shades of an Irish twilight, William and Edward returned to Tulira Castle. After a fine meal that reflected the excellent shooting of the gamekeeper, they retired to the billiard room. The room was one of dark, almost black wood. About the pool table were the heads of animals killed in the many safaris conducted through the centuries by the owners. The heads of lions, tigers and even a bear were displayed. The room had a faint odor of soot about it from the numerous fires from ages past.

"Edward, Augusta is far more attractive a woman than you have described. I believe you referred to her as a plain woman without distinguishing features; 'plain in dress and in features' is how I believe you put it. I too will, however, describe her as such if I am ever questioned. I have no need to contradict the judgment of a friend."

William continued, "I think, however, that you wanted to save her for yourself. I see her not as the model, but as the lovely component of the finished painting."

"William, you have observed something I have missed." Edward sighed.

"I find her very attractive in that her voice, mind and physical features are so distinctive. Her eyes, most of all, commanded my attention," added William.

Edward responded, "I can somewhat identify with you. I am afraid I never received the stare from her that you received. She is always looking away when she speaks to me. With you, it is different. I noticed that her eyes never left you. I can't imagine why," Edward said as the eight ball landed loudly in the center pocket. "You have completely distracted me. An easy shot royally missed."

Edward continued, "William, I was really shocked that you would suggest painting Lady Gregory. We all know Jack received the artistic legacy in your family. You are no more an artist than I am. Your gift is in your words. I doubt if you will ever have the courage to show her what you have painted. You have obviously found a way to enjoy her company for a prolonged period of time. But there will be an accounting, you know."

"Edward, my imaginative friend, it is true. It was my way of getting to spend more time with her. As you know, I enjoy painting landscapes, however modest my talent. I wanted to be sure she did not offer just a general invitation to paint the natural environment excluding her from attending."

"I must admit you have a strategy. What I can't figure out is why you feel so strongly about getting to know her better. After all, she is older than you, and you do have a weakness for beautiful women. I remember you endlessly dwelling upon the subject of Maud Gonne."

William laughed. "A sore subject indeed. Yes, I found Maud to be an exceptional beauty. In fact, since first seeing her at my father's studio in Dublin, I think that I have never ceased to be in love with her."

"Now, how long has that mystical love lasted, William?"

"I met her for the first time on 30 January 1889."

"I don't think I can remember the exact date of having met anyone." Edward laughed. "I doubt if you are that good with all dates. You definitely are a man who mistakes passion for love."

William responded, "It was cold that time in Dublin. In fact, it was miserable. When I walked into the parlor, I was dripping water on my mother's fine floor. Maud looked at me and said, 'Good sir, your glasses are even wearing raindrops.' Her hair was the color of a rose; her smile captured the rainbow above Galway Bay," William said as he rested the butt of the cue on the pool table. For a moment, he paused, staring out of the window into the light that fell softly upon the fields beyond the castle.

"Come on, Yeats. There you go again drifting into a world you alone can see. A beautiful woman, who I understand, has repeatedly rejected you as a lover. I heard one gentleman state that his wife had told him you had even proposed to Maud. Is it any wonder than another woman would look attractive to you? I was convinced you had a need for romance, nothing more. I am now convinced that you also have a need for rejection."

"Edward, I understand what you are saying. Yes, I do love her passionately and that love has not been returned, but there was something about Lady Gregory that was very different from Maud. In her voice, eyes and even in her wit, she far surpasses anyone I have ever met. From what little I know of her work, I feel that we are communicating even though not literally speaking; sharing impressions that are formed within our thoughts."

"Come on, Yeats, I know you are attracted to spiritualism, and some say, even to the occult. I seriously doubt if a person such as Lady Gregory even noticed you other than as a curiosity. I do have to admit, her landscapes are no better than your own. At least your mutual lack of talent in that one particular area may form a bond indeed," Edward said laughingly as he broke the next set of billiard balls.

That night, the castle had a chill to it that not even the peat fires could tame. The wind, from off Galway Bay, blew incessantly. The candle flame upon the nearby table pointed horizontally away from the window like a finger extended towards the door of the room as wax dripped upon the silver candlestick holder.

William could not sleep. The more he tried to enter the realm of Hypnos, the God of Sleep, the more he changed his position upon the four-poster bed. The flickering flame produced a shadow play upon the ceiling of the bed's canopy. He kept hearing Augusta's voice and seeing her image walking with him in a walled garden. The more the clock sounded the early hours of the morning, the more certain he was that she too was awake and thinking of him; their secret meeting within the woods of Coole.

❧ 6 ❧
Thoor Ballylee

Adjoining Lady Gregory's estate, flowed Coole River for which the house and grounds were named; a clear, fast running river of shallow depth except in the winter months when heavy rains from off the sea caused it to flood its banks. Along its winding course, a tall, four-story gray tower castle commanded the surrounding area. It was built by the de Burgo family in the 16th century; the family having established itself in Connacht after 1200.

Immense stone walls many feet thick insured that the defenders of the castle were safe against the tools of 16th century warfare. A narrow winding staircase connected the floors with small windows allowing but scant sunlight to enter. A murder hole above the main entryway to the castle enabled defenders to shoot arrows down onto the marauders. Inside, the walls were whitewashed to capture what little light managed to enter the fortification. Every design element of the tower was intended for defensive purposes and not for esthetic beauty.

The years had not been kind to Thoor Ballylee. Having lost its function as a fortification, it was allowed to deteriorate. Small birds claimed the pinions of the upper castle walls; other wild dwellers soon dwelt within its chambers.

The last occupants of the tower, an Irish farming family, had left an eclectic collection of furniture that included a homemade bed of rough-hewn wood, a dining table and an assortment of mismatched handmade chairs. Outside in the tall green grass, were a few remaining stacks of peat. Lady Gregory had previously sent a member of her staff to clean the room that had a view of the river and was located on the lower floor. A trunk held fine linen and an assortment of dishes. Bottles of wine were also provisioned in the event that a visitor in Coole Park might have an interest in spending a fortnight in seclusion.

Lady Gregory was often asked who would want to spend so much time alone. She would generally reply, "A person who desires to become acquainted with his own self." Baffled, few remaining questions were to be asked. Lady Gregory did not want to admit she was the one who sought the sanctuary of Thoor Ballylee after her husband's death four years earlier; her affair with Wilfrid having greatly affected her in so many ways. Even though their relationship had ended, she still dreamed of their time together in Egypt.

When she stayed at the castle, she would sit by the window facing the river. There on a wooden table in the dimming light, she would compose poetic images within her thoughts; words written not about her husband but about her lover.

As soon as Augusta would pen a verse, she would cast it into the fire. Secrets had to be hidden from all those present; even those not seen. The stone walls of the tower could shield her emotions just as it had protected the warrior in ages past. Augusta knew that she too needed walls of stone; strength to defend and the comfort of a protector.

As she looked at a small bird drinking from Coole River, her thoughts returned to Egypt. The market places selling fruits of every description; pomegranates, melons, oranges, grapes, peaches, mangoes and dates; their odors mixing in a bowl of humid, moist, warm air from off the Nile. She laughed as she thought of Wilfrid, and their attempts at making pomegranate wine; their mouths covered in the delicious fruit.

Not only did the fruits offer their scents, but the vegetables in the vendors' wooden cribs as well. Garlic, onions, tomatoes, and artichokes exhaled from the produce stands. As Augusta and Wilfrid walked past the small stores, shisha pipes filled the air of the streets with the rich, flavored tobaccos of Egypt.

She thought of the taste of salads served on beds of chipped ice brought from the nearby British ice plant by Wilfrid's staff; a trail of water falling from the block as the porter rapidly walked with the melting ice. "Funny, how odors, smells and sights can so easily be recalled in the silence of the darkened tower room," she spoke aloud to the silence.

"How cold the river seems even in the warmth of a summer day," Augusta thought as she watched leaves making their hurried passage towards the sea often colliding with the river's stones that rose like markers for the dead.

"It was foolish of me to have flirted with Mr. Yeats on my first having met him. From his appearance, he is a few years younger than I and very handsome. He must think me to be a desperate old woman seeking his attention. It is only my position that could possibly attract him to me. Edward had earlier said that he had fallen in love with a woman named 'Maud Gonne' who is young and beautiful; very close to his age. Why would he want to paint me? Perhaps to flatter me?"

She looked at the small gold watch that she carried pinned to her lapel. "It is getting late; the early morning hours have arrived too soon. I must return to Coole Park and await his arrival."

⚛ 7 ⚛

The Painting

He opened both the shutters and windows of his room. The morning was clear and filled with the scent of garden and meadow. William felt young, alive and thankful even though he had found it very difficult to sleep; yet he could not purge himself of Maud Gonne. She continued to dwell within his thoughts regardless of whether he was awake or asleep.

As he stepped from the castle's stone stairs, Edward called, "William, you forgot your new canvases."

The walk to Lady Gregory's was enjoyable. While crossing over the bridges on his way, he leaned against the warm stone walls looking down into the rapidly flowing waters. He watched water spiders chase one another in the quieter pools where hungry trout waited for the return of the cool time of the day when shades would play upon the bottom of the stream. Dragonflies clung to flowering plants and rested upon lily pads in the quiet pools. His thoughts moved as rapidly as the small discarded leaves that fled beneath the bridge.

He especially enjoyed the mystery of the turloughs of Coole Park; their froth-rimmed basins and vanishing waters that reappear with the fall rains. He loved the odors of the herbs and wild flowers that grew by them; yellow flowers, meadow rue and marsh orchids were in abundance as were the hums of myriad bees and other insects that enjoyed the warm day. Occasional, the smell of mint drifted upon the gentle wind.

Even though many of the turloughs were now free of their water, some still contained frogs, newts and fairy shrimps. Enjoying the feast of the well-spread table were white-fronted geese, teal and whooper swans. So beautiful were the swans that he intended to later immortalize them on canvas.

He thought about his exchange with Augusta the other day, and how much they shared in such a short time. William also thought about Augusta as a woman. He liked strong, intelligent women who merited his treatment of them as equals. A woman of power with both land and title was to be much admired, if not envied. Her earnest familiarity with him was most appealing. She had been so forthcoming that it almost disarmed him. While Maud was only able to disappoint, Lady Gregory could overwhelm.

William rested once more upon the stone abutment of the last bridge before Coole Park. He placed his easel and artist box upon the railing as well. He closed his eyes so that he sensed only the warmth of the sun. William felt within his heart that the next few steps he took to the entryway of Coole Park house were to be life altering.

Augusta saw him from her library window as he rested upon the bridge. She admired his thick black hair, scholarly dress and height. As he once again started walking towards the house, she looked again at her reflection in the window.

Soon William had arrived at the main entryway. The doorbell sounded and a staff member opened the heavy wooden doors.

"Good day, sir. Lady Gregory is expecting you in the drawing room."

William followed her doorman, Henry, as he walked into a room of immense size. The chamber was appointed in many couches of exquisite fabrics of bright colors; aqua, orange and violet. Paintings from Paris hung upon the walls. There Lady Gregory stood like an adornment within a Victorian garden; her white full-length skirt providing contrast to the large palms and other exotic plants that grew in the filtered sun of the Victorian garden's skylight.

"Lady Gregory, what a pleasure to see you."

"It is nice seeing you today, William. Would you care for some tea and scones?" she said with a smile. Since a staff member was present, she ignored his formal use of her title.

"Yes, that would be nice. Even though the sun is brilliant, the air is still cool. Some tea before our outing would be most pleasant," he said, unable to remove his eyes from her. "From your exhibits, I see that you like the Impressionist. They are, in the art world, considered to be both modern and controversial."

"You are correct," Augusta responded. "I must admit I was more a fan of realism, but then the paintings of Renoir especially captured my attention. I think him not to be as radical as Monet. Renoir's images, while dreamy, are more realistic. The expressions of his subjects convey their emotions. The artist allows us to look within; perhaps to see the soul of the model."

"I think not," replied William. "The artists permit us to look into the moment. The model is but a fragment of the time captured."

"During my last visit to Paris," William continued, "I enjoyed looking at an exhibit that featured the works of Pissarro, Morisot, Cassatt and Renoir. I see from your collection that you do favor Renoir. The breath of his subjects does include both that which is conventional as well as debatable." He spoke while observing a masterpiece of Renoir's that featured a beautiful, young woman bathing. "He is also able to express natural beauty without appealing to prurient interest."

Augusta responded, "Who is our judge? I look upon every act within life to be both beautiful and meaningful. My son Robert, as well as my own strolls about Coole Park, has taught me that we are our only judge." As she spoke, she looked towards a painting of her husband, Sir Gregory. The painting showed a man of heavy size with his hand resting upon a globe. Behind him through a window, could be seen elephants carrying large logs within their trunks. Sir Gregory's apparel was uniform-like in appearance.

"William, I noticed you are staring at Sir Gregory. That painting was done while he was Governor of Ceylon by a local artist. I have never been able to make out the artist's name. I wish I could have known Sir Gregory then. India has always seemed so distant from Ireland, yet by steamship, it is not that far away; perhaps a month or so voyage.

"Lady Gregory, you do have a great collection of art. I am always pleased to see artistic works spread throughout the world. We never know when turmoil may return to Europe and with it, the destruction of our culture.

Increasingly, the Kaiser's speeches are more warlike in nature."

"I agree with you, Europe has never known a lasting peace," she added. "I am afraid that it may also be said of our own country. Right here in Ireland, there is more and more call for land reform and for an end to English oversight. People like William O'Brien are calling for a redistribution of land ownership. We can only pray that any reform that takes place will be reasonable, peaceful and honorable. We must learn to compromise."

"If Ireland goes the way of revolution, all of our country's art will be threatened. The Irish must be taught about the beauty of their own culture. It will be our duty as patriots to provide a pathway for a peaceful reformation if conflict does indeed take place," replied William.

"Mr. Yeats, to whom do you owe your allegiance?"

"I have never thought about such a clear division of choice. I have never seen things in opposites."

"What a safe answer," she replied. "That is certainly not quote worthy. I must assume that you are a survivalist."

"You judge me wrong, madam. When choices are clear, I will make my decision regarding with whom I will stand."

"Even though I understand the difficulties of the poor, I would hate to see the woods of Coole Park cut down and made into firewood. Thank goodness, the turloughs cannot be harvested for they harbor only disappearing waters. They are ever renewing like life itself."

William replied, "I would hate to see even one of these fine beech trees cut. You also have a beautiful mixture of oak, ash, hazel, elm and yew. The heat of burning wood is only temporary."

"You amaze me. The majority of my visitors are not familiar with even the most common of trees. If I continue to be impressed, I will ask you to carve your name on the copper beech in my garden. I think your friend Edward may have already attempted to carve something on my tree. I will need to look for myself to see what, if anything, he has inscribed. He does not understand that the tree will heal itself and with that healing, his words will disappear."

A moment of silence occurred, and then abruptly, William said, "Augusta, with your permission, please select a location for me to paint. I am so looking forward to being outside on such a lovely day. I think nature has no intention of holding us bound inside dark chambers when such beauty surrounds us. Let us replace the smell of peat with that of the rose."

"Have we not already agreed upon Shan-walla?" She did not realize that his question was one of courtesy only.

William had left his artist box and easel outside the front doors. Her staff members, Ann and Phillip were to carry not only his art materials but also a large picnic basket accompanied by blankets. In addition, there was a carafe of fine wine in Ann's hand.

As they walked, Augusta would occasionally smile at him. He knew at that moment he had found a friend he wished to keep. No other woman had interested him so profoundly in so many ways. Both physically and mentally, he saw her as the ideal acquaintance; a person with whom he could converse with on a wide variety of subjects without insisting that he agree with her opinions. His creativity depended not upon conformity but upon challenging himself to explore his own emotional observations. The warmth of her smile and mannerisms created a physical beauty he had not known before.

It then occurred to Augusta that he was only being courteous in his suggestion of Shan-walla as a location to paint since it was close to her house. Augusta asked, "Did you not mention earlier a favored place to paint? I thought I recalled you saying so."

"May I change my mind? I did walk past Kyle-dortha. The wild ducks and abundant shade should provide both interest and comfort."

"How did you know the name of the wood?" she asked.

"Edward mentioned it to me. He loves to walk your estate since there is such a diversity of flora and fauna to be found."

Augusta took his arm and laughed. "You are so academic for such a young man. Are you ever not serious; did youth flee so early?"

He returned her smile as he tripped over a small branch that was hidden in the tall, soft meadow grass. "You see, when I want to be humorous, I am reminded of my mortality; this time by a stick of your wood."

The journey to the shore of Kyle-dortha was but a comfortable distance. The lake was not yet dry in that rains had managed to keep it reasonably full for the time of year. Small frogs in the tall grass leaped at their approach. In the still waters, fairy shrimp could still be seen swimming. A large swan rode effortlessly under the overhanging limbs of a large oak tree. Birds sang loudly both within the meadow and deep within the forest adjacent to the turlough. Pondweeds, watercress and aquatic buttercups lived upon or near to its surface.

"Ann and Phillip, please spread the blanket under the large oak closest to the bank of the lake," she said with a motion of her hand.

As Augusta reclined on the brilliantly colored blanket, William set up his easel and positioned his paints and brushes. He arranged his colors according to their hues. His emotions were complex; the warm sunlight upon his skin gave him both peace and pleasure. The myriad sounds of the small lake assured him of the presence of abundant life regardless of the form that it had taken. A Beautiful

Demoiselle flew about them as they looked upon the waters of the lake.

The greatest source of his creative drive, however, was the presence of Augusta. She had let down her hair and it now rested upon her shoulders. It was as though a monarch butterfly had emerged from its cocoon; her hair catching the fleeing light that moved in and out of the leafy shadows. At first she rested on her elbow in a reclining position, then switched to rest upon a large pillow that Ann placed beneath her head. She turned her body towards him and smiled. "You are so meticulous with your oils; each labeled and in the same exact position. Please tell me, do you write like you organize your paints?"

"Augusta, may I assume you intend me a compliment?" He then paused. "Does art exist in that which is random? I see a great cohesiveness in nature and, therefore, in its artistic expression."

Augusta noticed how he observed everything about him. He would pause momentarily upon various objects as though attempting to understand their meaning. She sensed that words were being created yet to be spoken.

"You have the mannerisms of a feral cat. Each movement directs your attention to it," she said as she smiled.

"I will agree with you. Every movement represents something new to me. Do you see and hear the myriad wild bees as they dart from flower to flower in search of the fragrance therein? Why is one flower chosen over another? There are so many questions I seek answers to."

He continued, "May I paint you as I would this meadow and all within it that is natural?"

"How would you like for me to pose?" she asked.

"As you are at this very moment."

"In that I am reclining, I fear that I may sleep," she said with a smile.

"I will paint then a portrait of your contentment. I would like to think that you find peace in my presence. What greater gift is there to give? The wild honey is already made for us. There is no table to be set or silver to polish. There are no flowers to be cut since they grow so freely about us."

The warm sun relaxed her body. She knew that he had given her permission to be herself without restraints or conditions. There was no demand placed upon her to be a conversationalist; an artist of words. The young man had given her a gift beside the still waters of Kyle-dortha. She, like King David, now rested totally content in his presence.

The evening fell upon Coole Park as they return to the house of Sir Gregory. The owls had not yet sounded within the seven woods.

"Augusta, I hope you found our day to be enjoyable."

"William, you have not yet shown me the painting. How am I to judge whether you are a great artist or a struggling beginner?" she said coquettishly.

"I am afraid I would embarrass us both if I were to do so."

"William, I am having some guests for tomorrow evening that you might like to meet. We will have dinner, drinks and then a séance. You are a spiritual person. I would think that such an event might prove of interest to you."

"Are you inviting some people that I might know?"

"I don't think so except for Edward."

"Yes, I accept your invitation.

☙ 8 ❧

The Séance

A light rain was falling when William and Edward arrived at Coole Park. William was very interested in the quest for the spiritual. He was by nature not interested in formal religions that required a strict obedience to a set of written rules or codes. He felt, instead, that each individual was a faith unto himself, and as such, would receive individual communications from that which exists beyond this life. As such, he was more than eager to meet Martha Fuller O'Brien.

The doorman took their hats and large woolen coats that shed water as they removed them. Another staff member led them into the large parlor that glowed with candles and fireside light. In the center of the large mahogany table were three candles grasped by a single silver candleholder.

"William, I would like for you to meet Mrs. O'Brien. She will be conducting the meeting," said Augusta.

William took her hand and lightly kissed it. "Mrs. O'Brien, it is a pleasure to meet you." He observed that she was a lady, like Augusta, in her mid to late forties. She was of less stature than Augusta and heavier in weight. He was to later find out that her family had fallen upon difficult times as both her father and grandfather had gambled away their estates.

Mrs. O'Brien's black velvet dress was animated in a variety of colorful stones; the colors sparkling with the changing light. About her neck hung a large silver medallion that William did not recognize, in the shape of a pentagon; upon its surface were three small pyramids.

The meal was served in the formal dining room; a large space with dark, unlit corners. Three staff members positioned themselves to serve the guests who included not only William and Edward but Professor Haynes formerly of Trinity University, Mrs. Evelyn O'Malley from one of the nearby estates, and Miss Maud Phillips.

After proper introductions, the visitors were seated; before them rested the sterling silver vessels holding the eight-course meal. Steam rose from the serving trays into the cool moist air of the room. The sounds of meat being carved and dishes passed between guest infiltrated the quietness of the room. Glasses spoke as wine was poured into the crystal vessels. As the meal ended, fancy cakes and preserved fruit were shared. The sweetest of carefully selected wines followed the desert while hot tea simmered within their cups. Only quiet self-censored conversation took place between the guests.

At the conclusion of the meal, the parties to the séance where invited into an adjacent parlor where they sat down before a large circular, dark wooden table of ornate design; the uniqueness of the monkey carvings indicated that it had come from Ceylon or perhaps Bombay.

Soon each member took the other's hand. Every other candle that had provided only a faint glow upon the walls was blown out. Ms. O'Brien spoke after a moment of silence. "Is there someone present in this room that wishes to speak to us?" Only silence replied. Then she called more loudly, "Is there someone present in this room that wishes to speak to us?"

William could feel the hands of Mrs. O'Malley and Professor Haynes tightening. He continued to approach the séance in doubt of its validity. Lending credence to the event was the personality of Lady Gregory. She was not the kind to be misled by a charlatan.

Then Mrs. O'Brien began to sway gently from side to side while her eyes were transfixed on the plaster medallion from which the chandelier extended. She remained not speaking, yet she was apparently in a trance. All the guests and attending staff stared at her waiting for words to flow from her mouth. Again only silence was uttered.

Then without warning she began to speak to the guests in a voice that was not her own. It was lower pitched than her previously heard voice.

"There in the castle two lovers sleep while twilight falls upon the field and meadow pond.
"Two lovers kiss and are alone.
"Betraying and betrayed they cling like ivy upon the stone.
"Two lives invite a third; a love taken to be revealed."

Mrs. O'Brien appeared to suddenly shake herself awake. Those in attendance lightly applauded her performance. William noticed slight perspiration about her lips even though the room had grown cold.

"Is there to be more?" asked William whose interest in her words had greatly amused him. "Am I to assume this is a riddle from the other side?"

Augusta looked first at Mrs. O'Brien and then at William. "Mrs. O'Brien appears to be exhausted. When a person looks into another world, the journey is both physically and psychologically demanding. I doubt she even remembers what has just transpired.

William looked at all the guests. "What do the words mean? Is it the present or the future that she has visited? I admit my curiosity has been greatly aroused."

Mrs. O'Brien appeared to be surprised by the question. "You must tell me what happened."

"Madam, you were apparently in a trance during the séance," replied William. "There is no clear answer to give you. You presented us a riddle with few clues."

❧ 9 ❧
An Invitation to Remain

After the other guests had excused themselves for the evening, only William and Edward remained. Edward had found the wine and cognac to be of excellent vintage. Seldom had William enjoyed so great an evening.

Edward nodded towards him. "William, you can stay as late as you like, but I am going home. A fine meal and stimulating conversation has truly capped an outstanding evening."

Augusta replied while looking at William, "If you like and are in the mood, please do stay and have another decanter with me. From Edward, I understand that you enjoy sherry. I must admit the hour is late, but there is still so much to discuss. If you agree, I will later have one of my staff members take you home in the carriage."

William found himself in an uncomfortable situation. He longed to stay but the fatigue of a long day wore heavily upon him. He paused, and then suddenly aware of a deep unspoken desire, he said, "Lady Gregory, I cannot refuse so great an offer." At that moment, he felt like a trout of Coole River, unable to refuse the temptation placed before him.

"So be it. Let's move closer to the fire," Augusta said quietly. "It is always amazing that these large houses are so cold that we do not get to enjoy them except in isolated areas near the flame. In the winter months, a squatter's shack provides the same space for conversation." Her eyes followed his movements as he moved his chair closer to the hearth and to her.

"I understand that Sir Gregory was married before you two met?" William asked.

"Yes, that is true. His wife died prior to our becoming acquainted. Her name was Elizabeth Bowdoin. She had been married previously to James Bowdoin who died before she met Sir Gregory. Elizabeth had been dead seven or eight years prior to Sir Gregory and myself becoming friends."

"I am afraid I am not acquainted with the Bowdoin family," stated William.

"Perhaps you knew of Sir William Clay. That was her father. He was of the landed class."

"Yes, I do recall having heard his name while I was visiting in London. I never, however, had an opportunity to meet him."

Augusta smiled towards William. "You would have liked Sir Gregory. He, like you, filled a room with his presence. He was very active politically which meant that he had the opportunity to meet the most interesting people. He was a Dubliner having been born in the Castle in Dublin's Phoenix Park. In addition to his political career, he was a writer."

"What type of writing did he do?" asked William.

"Mainly political essays; like all cultured gentlemen, he also wrote poetry. Yes, mainly love poems."

"Someday, you will have to share the poems with me," William said.

Their eyes followed the freed embers as they accompanied the smoke rising in the hearth.

"Were you happy with Sir Gregory?" William asked as he sipped from a glass of his preferred sherry.

"Yes, I was. Perhaps I was too eager to enjoy life. Unlike me, he was content with his accomplishments."

"You have everything; yet you are discontented?" questioned William.

"Our mortality brings discontentment. We have so little time," Augusta said softly.

At that moment and purely without intent, he reached over and rested his hand upon hers. It was a touch of compassion. Augusta looked quickly at him and then away. At first she intended to remove his light clasp upon her hand yet she hesitated. "Why," she thought, "should I not be touched at this late hour of the night? My husband is dead and I am breaking no rules in my own home in having my hand held innocently; so lightly touched by a brilliant young man with whom I share so many things."

William and Augusta allowed their hands to continue to rest upon her lap. Her hand felt very cold to him while she enjoyed the warmth and reassurance of his touch. They sat there silently as the wood burned brightly and then turned into blues and reds. The staff had gone to bed much earlier. Only the ticking clock and the sighing of the hearth were to be heard.

"I want to share a special place with you," said Augusta.

"This is a very special place to me," William responded.

"No, this room is not what I am referring to. On the border of my property, as you know, is Coole River. There is a tower castle located there next to the bank of the river. You probably never noticed it on your walks; the trees hide it so effectively this time of the year."

"You are correct, I don't remember seeing a tower in my walks; but again, I have not walked over your entire park. Please tell me more about it."

"It is where I go when I want to write or to be alone. It is a place of contrast to me. The stone endures the changing seasons while the meadow flowers will not last beyond the frost; only to lay buried in the snows that follows. I see beauty in both. Which William is most like you, the stone or meadow flower?"

"Augusta, you have given me a riddle to solve that is more of the late hour and drink than of sobriety. Being a polite and thankful guest, I will answer your question even though it may tarnish your opinion of me." William paused before responding further. "My writing is like the stone that endures, if the critics allow, while my adoration of you is more like the flowers within the meadow. Our relationships are temporary yet beauty exists within the moment. What comfort will stone provide? Yet your soft hand gives me solace."

Augusta smiled. "You have answered my question very well. Tomorrow afternoon, I will take you and you alone to my tower. I will have the staff prepare it for your grand arrival."

⇜10⇝
⸝ord 𝒲illington

William knew he was not the only suitor for Augusta's love. There had been talk in Dublin about another man much older than Lady Gregory that had also become infatuated with her. Lord Willington lived nearby on a landed estate in a Palladian house of immense proportions. His infatuation with Augusta had always dwelt within his mind since first seeing her as a young woman, yet he had failed to act after her husband's death, fearing her rejection. After all, he was keenly aware that he was many years her senior.

Lord Willington was very much aware that Lady Gregory's husband had also been much older than her. Other than his wealth and land, he knew he could not compete with the brilliant young men that seemed to flock to Coole Park; yet his love for her continued to dwell deep within his heart. He believed that had he openly revealed his desire, that he would have been summarily dismissed, yet he longed for an opportunity to confess his feelings.

His thoughts, regardless of the season, often ventured to Coole Park. One day in early spring, Alfred Willington decided to walk to Coole Park for a reason that he later could not fully understand. He felt invigorated by a day of warmth and brilliant sun. In his walk, he could only hope to see Augusta since he had not received a formal invitation to her house.

As he rounded the corner stone wall of her formal garden, he peered within. There before him was Augusta delicately cutting roses. Next to her was a staff member dutifully holding a wicker basket into which Augusta placed the long stem roses being careful not to wound herself on a thorn.

Augusta immediately sensed the presence of another. Turning about, she said, "Good morning, Lord Willington. I did not expect to see you on such a lovely day. I did not hear your carriage approaching the house. My dogs did not bark so they must consider you a welcomed intruder to my garden."

"Lady Gregory, I chose to walk this morning rather than to take my carriage. I understand that a long stroll is good for the constitution. The more I walked, the closer I came to Coole Park. I could not then excuse myself from having failed to say 'good morning' to you."

"I agree with your decision to visit with me. How are things at Willington Hall? I hope your sister is feeling better." Alfred's sister, Margareta, had sustained an injury as a result of a fall during a steeplechase event. Her plunge from the horse's back had left her partially paralyzed. She had been a beautiful young lady highly sought by gentlemen throughout County Galway. Before the injury, there was talk of her impending engagement to the son of a wealthy landowner.

"Augusta, Margareta is doing well. I think the fine weather has made all us feel much better. She, like you, is enjoying her garden. The smell of roses and the sound of splashing water reinvigorates us all."

"Alfred, I agree with her choice of pleasures. I know my rose bushes have missed the sun during the last few days of heavy rains. No matter where I travel, even to Egypt with my late husband, I have never seen roses so vivid in color as these Irish flowers. It must be our fine soil that nourishes such delightful bouquets."

"Yes, the flowers love the soil, sun and rains of Ireland. It heightens the intense color and increases the fragrances within our gardens." The garden was alive with many varieties of plants and ornamental shrubs. Lord Willington, like many of the landed classes, also enjoyed collecting specimens of insects to be displayed within his study. He could not help but notice the hum of the many honeybees and the erratic flights of the Beautiful Demoiselle dragonflies that were congregating about the small decorative ponds in the process of mating. Their unique blue green body and iridescent veins fascinated Alfred. He, like many Victorian gentlemen, was well read regarding Darwin's theory of evolution. He could not, however, understand why, other than for the pleasure of man, such a magnificent insect had evolved.

"Augusta, it is good to be alive this day. I feel much younger than my years should allow." Though his heart desired her, he was afraid to express the words he longed to say. Even though he had been knighted for his daring military leadership during various Boer War campaigns, he felt afraid in her presence. He knew he wanted to say so much more than mere pleasantries.

"I wish you would come more often to Willington House," said Alfred. "You know how much Margareta appreciates and enjoys your visits. I cannot, of course, deny that I do as well."

Augusta sensed that he was withholding much greater feelings than he was willing to admit to her. She looked at him with a strong, fixed stare. "I must confess I have spent many pleasant hours in both Margareta and your company. You have known me all of my adult life. How could we not be friends?"

Alfred nervously cut a rose with a small penknife and handed it to her. "May this rose express my feelings towards you," said Alfred without making eye contact. Augusta quickly took the brilliantly red and fragrant rose from him and let it drop into the basket without speaking a word. Only her gesture spoke to him of her true feelings.

Augusta did not want to outwardly show how she felt about him. She admired his dedication to Queen Victoria and the British Empire. His valor on the fields of battle was indeed unquestionable. She even admired how straight he stood in his uniform yet today, in the bright sun in common apparel, he appeared a much smaller man; perhaps even older than she had remembered. She sensed that in her presence, he was not a leader but a follower awaiting her to command or even to commit him to action. Augusta imagined that since Lord Gregory had been a much older man than her, that Alfred had assumed that age did not matter, but on this beautiful day, it did.

Before her was a contrast that seemed to be overpowering. She thought of the restless youthfulness of William and the stoic proper Lord Willington. "What foolishness," she thought, "that an unknown poet could be admired and possibly loved more than the man who stood before her." She knew within her heart that passion was not akin to reasonable action.

"Augusta, walk with me beyond your garden. This morning I saw on one of your turloughs a most unusual swan. It was pure black with eyes the color of rubies. When I first saw it, I thought it might belong to the fairies." Alfred knew of Lady Gregory's interest in the myths of rural Ireland. He desperately needed to justify any attention he gave to her.

Augusta knew such a swan did not exist on her estate for she had visited each turlough on numerous occasions. She further reasoned that such a swan probably did not even exist in nature At this moment, she realized she must make a decision, yet she hesitated for fear of offending a dear friend. "Yes, let's walk," she uttered quickly avoiding any eye contact.

They walked slowly out of the garden and towards the east where tall billowing clouds reflected the sun as though dressed in gowns of radiant glow. Before them were the seven woods and the turloughs of the estate. The hedges and fields were ornate with their flowering crowns of vivid almost shimmering colors.

As they paused under a large, ancient beech tree, Alfred straightened his posture as though addressing his command. "Augusta, you know I have always loved you. Even when I knew I had no chance to win your heart, I sought you within my thoughts. Please forgive a man whose desires cannot be met. I realize that too much separates us, but could you love me for only a moment. Lie to me if you must but let me offer you more than the token of friendship this brief hour before the clouds return to Galway Bay, and the silence of my life is resumed."

Augusta spoke as she looked directly at him. "Alfred, my much-admired and kind friend, I think too much of you to lead you into believing that I can be more than a friend to you. I know of no one I have greater admiration for."

"Augusta, is it but age that separates us?" Lord Willington asked.

"Shall I mislead you and offer you hope? I cannot be that person, for if I am anything, it is that I am truthful. I do not merit your affection. My heart alone must be my guide for love; it cannot be an object of propriety. It does not listen to the accountant or to the commands of another. Perhaps the heart knows not reason yet it must pursue as the bee does the flower."

Alfred took her hand and held it lightly within his own. "My lovely person, I understand. I could only hope that you would accept me as more than a friend, but I am a great respecter of truthfulness. Though years will separate us from this moment, can we still remain friends?"

"Until we die," she responded.

☙11☙
The Dream

Arriving back at the Edward's estate, the castle seemed unusually chilled. The rain continued to fall as William arrived exhausted. The fires had died out in the many rooms and a profound quietness existed throughout the house.

After climbing into bed, he stared at the canopy above his head until his eyes closed. A dreamscape entered abruptly into his thoughts...

The great house sits isolated upon the moors; the wind blows strong as William, dressed in a full-length black coat, approaches it as one might view an image within a mirror; his hair tossed by the strength of the wind.

William intends to knock on the door but finds that it opens without so much as the turning of a knob. There before him is Lady Gregory dressed in a thin white gown with highly embroidered neck and sleeves. She is reclining upon a red velvet settee within her parlor.

"Come, set by my side," Lady Gregory says as she turns to look out the chamber window. Outside, towering black clouds are moving in from the sea.

After having removed his overcoat, William sits down on the settee in a relaxed pose and takes her hand, kissing it lightly as she smiles.

"Are we to be lovers?" she asks.

Outside are the loud angry shouts of many voices. Both William and Augusta look towards the windows. A large crowd of peasants has gathered outside the house. Their shouts penetrate the thick walls of the room. They then begin to chant, "The Land for the Irish People! The Land for the Irish People!"

"William, just ignore them," Augusta said softly. She pulls him down to kiss his lips. Soon her hands run through his wind-tossed hair.

So involved are they in passion that they do not notice red leaves blowing in from the open windows and doors. Soon the leaves adorn the lovers like garments cast by the wind. A loud explosion is heard as flames begin to devour the chamber walls; paintings fall to the floor as their frames are rent asunder. William sees the painting of the Nile burning before him.

He raises himself upon one shoulder to see the Coole Park beginning to be engulfed in flames. Outside the peasants are laughing and mocking them, "Now the English will go home! Now the English will go home!"

Lady Gregory does not react to the violence taking place but pulls him down once more upon her.

William awakened to the sounds of late morning.

A staff member knocked on the heavy wood door of his bed chamber. "Good morning, sir. Breakfast will be served within the hour."

At first, William could not identify what was real. Startled, he arose thinking the castle itself was aflame only to realize he had a nightmare. The wood smoke from the fireplace in the great hall had penetrated under his chamber door for the fire had been lit early before his awakening.

Breakfast was served in the dining room of the castle; a room of dark wood walls and tall glass windows that looked out upon the courtyard. Even though the voice of nature was just beyond the glass, it was a room of silence.

Eggs, tomatoes, bacon, a variety of breads, puddings and fruits were placed upon the table. Steaming cups of breakfast tea were also presented to the guests. Napkins rolled tightly about the silverware added to the formality of the room.

"William, I hope you are not too exhausted. Lady Gregory certainly does not live by the timepiece of others. There are nights, so I am told, when she does not go to bed at all," said Edward. "Some would have us believe it is the sign of a troubled soul, while others would say it is but her nature."

"What could there possibly be to keep her awake? Her husband has been dead now four years. Her son Robert seems to be in perfect health. Her lands and house are secure," said William.

Edward replied, "Only rumors, but I think she still has not resolved herself to Sir Gregory's death. I base this in part on the fact that she continues to dress in black when seen in public. I know of no one, except Queen Victoria, that has continued to wear the colors of mourning for such a lengthy period of time."

"Edward, to be honest, I did not notice what Lady Gregory was wearing last evening. The color of her dress was not obvious in either the candle or firelight. Why do you think she continues to mourn?"

"It is commonly told that the Lady had met a young poet while in Egypt. Their relationship was later to develop into an affair. I believe his name was Wilfrid Blunt; a British type with connections to society through his wife. She was somehow related to Lord Byron. It seems like our Wilfrid has always been attracted to wealthy women since he had financial concerns that only a well-bred wife could solve."

William laughed. "You can't be serious. The woman I met is not that type at all. To me, she's somewhat mousy;

dressed plainly; too old for a lover and was not attractive. In fact, the charms I've noted are her strength, intelligence and kindness. I would have assumed that she would have immediately discerned the less than noble intent of Mr. Blunt." William knew he was not truthful in expressing his observations to Edward. He too had become infatuated with her many charms. William did not wish to share her many attributes with Edward for fear that he might become attracted to her. Their estates were in close proximity and such a marriage would benefit them both financially.

"William, you are an innocent. You do not realize it, but you have described exactly what a man most desires in a woman. If she is overly attractive, she will not be attentive to her husband. If she is strong, she will not leave him when his wealth has deserted them both. If she is intelligent, she will be in a position to advise him. Lastly, if she is kind, she will tolerate his ever increasing faults."

"Edward, sage advice related to what I should look for in the fulfillment of my own desires. What say you to the age difference? Surely you cannot support that as a positive factor."

"William, you are a poet with many gifts of reasoning. Yet, you have failed to realize that age provides both variety and clarity to life? Wisdom sprouts not from youth but from the experience of having lived the emotions essential to a poet's creativity. Who better to read your words with comprehension than an older woman? Augusta is far from being too old to be a lover."

"Edward, as usual, you confound me at every turn. You confuse me. Why have you not sought her?"

Edward looked towards William as he spoke. "I have a fortune and a great estate. What need I of such a woman? It is true she would make any man a great companion. I, however, trust solely in myself. I do not need someone to be my conscience or my guide. I merely tell my servant when I want to go and all is arranged. Why should I seek someone who, with years, would demand that I ask permission of her? I am content and expect to grow old in such a condition." He smiled at William. "Besides my friend, I can purchase in Dublin what I desire. Is not every man and woman bought and sold?"

As the staff waited upon them, William could not help but remember the infatuation experienced within his dream. Even though Edward was correct in his objective, unemotional, description of her physical attributes, he could not forget the passion he felt for her even if it were only imaginary. What was it about this woman that could ferment such desire within Wilfrid, Lord Willingham and himself? "Strength, intelligence and kindness," were the most probable answers to his question. Yet her silent voice spoke of the sensuality within; both eyes and lips to command desire.

As William ate his breakfast, he stared out the window at two brightly colored finches that were pruning one another on a pear tree branch. William realized he did not have the time for a pointless affair even with a great lady of position. Yet he knew that reason was not akin to passion or to the affairs of the heart.

✌︎12✌︎
The Tower

Broken clouds moved across the sky of County Galway. Having both slept and eaten a hearty breakfast, William felt full of energy and was filled with excitement regarding his visit to see Lady Gregory. Upon stepping from the castle into the warm sunlight, he inhaled deeply; feeling a new sense of optimism and health.

The carriage awaited him in front of the castle. Edward had provided it as well as two coachmen to take William to the gate of Coole Park.

Rather than being taken directly to the house, he preferred that morning to walk from the gatehouse of Coole Park. Flowing water was musically colliding with stones within the streambeds as he sauntered towards the house. Meadowlarks sang in the clearings while ducks sounded the woodland alarm as they took to wing. Squirrels in the aged oaks ignored his presence as they chatted amongst themselves. As he walked, his shoes quickly became moist from having stepped into several small puddles between the exposed stones of the drive.

As he neared the house, peat fires were emitting gray smoke even though the morning was warm. He walked up the steps and sounded the bell.

"Good morning, sir. I hope you had a pleasant walk," the doorman said as he opened the heavy paneled doors.

"Outstanding indeed; the weather is perfect for a stroll," William answered.

"Please follow me to the parlor. Lady Gregory is preparing for your walk and is not yet ready to receive you."

Having made the journey from the entryway to the parlor, William then walked over to the large painting of Egypt that hung about the mantel. He thought how the same image had appeared within his dream the night before.

It was difficult to make out the artist's name even though it appeared to be signed 'WB.' The painting showed a British colonial home surrounded by formal gardens and orchards. Large exotic birds were walking about the yard. The pyramids could be seen in the distance. As he looked at the painting, he wondered if 'WB' could be the signature of Wilfrid Blunt.

William felt sadness as he thought about his own failed relationships with women. Throughout his life, he had been attracted to a variety of women who quickly tired of him. Perhaps he intentionally desired the companionship of those who would eventually reject and, therefore, hurt him. William reasoned at times that their rejection of him created the necessary suffering essential to his poetic creativity. He believed the brevity of life created the beauty to be found within it. Why not so the relationship between a man and a woman?

He remembered his attraction to his distant cousin, Laura Armstrong; a beautiful woman of great intellect. She was three years older than he and already engaged at the time of their meeting. Even though he knew inwardly that their relationship could not endure, he was attracted to her and quickly fell in love. Their relationship lasted barely two years before she eventually married her patiently waiting fiancée. Those two years were filled with passionate letters and promises that could not to be fulfilled.

Seven years earlier he had met Maud Gonne. Even though she expressed little interest in his flirtations, he felt a great attraction towards her. It was her inattention to him that drew William into the pursuit of her unreturned love.

"Good morning, William," said Augusta in a quiet, almost distant, voice. She appeared silently like a shadow cast upon a wall.

"Good morning, Lady Gregory."

"You make me feel so old when you say that. I do admit I am several years older than you; for that I must ask your forgiveness," Augusta said with an apologetic expression.

"'Forgiveness,' a strange word to use in conjunction with that which is unavoidable. Age gives us the ability to judge what we have done in the past. It, therefore, is our greatest guide to the future," said William having immediately remembered the words of Edward regarding his potential relationship with Lady Gregory.

"Our day trip has been carefully planned. I hope it will meet with your approval," said Augusta.

"I have no doubt you have attended to every detail," said William with a broad smile that conveyed the warmth of his growing affection. An affection he did not want to express too openly.

"I told my staff not to expect us back until late in the evening. That way, they will not worry about me," Augusta replied.

"You have great trust in me, Augusta. Your staff is very protective of you," William said as he moved closer to her.

As they walked towards the tower, Augusta adjusted the wrap about her shoulders. No longer was she wearing black but a full-length dress of bright red linen. The sun felt warm upon their cheeks and added to the pleasantness of the moment. As they walked upon uneven grown, he placed her arm within his own. Soon the path they followed led them into one of the seven woods of Coole.

"Please tell me about the tower we are walking towards. The stones from which they are built bear the scars of both glaciers and the flames of creation. I love the history of our land though it is written in the suffering of our people."

"It is, as you may know, a tower castle built in the 15th century. It is located adjacent to Coole River for which my estate is named," Augusta responded.

"I have always dreamed of owning such a castle," William said. "Literature is filled with stories set in such dwellings. I think of the authors and poets that have been inspired by the many towers that dot our land and the history they represent. Within my own mind, I see them as still occupied by those that dwelt within the past centuries."

"I agree with you, William. Whether they be castles or simple houses, they are not plaster and stone, but living emblems of their owners. It is a symbiotic relationship between two living things."

William responded, "I love how warm the sun feels. I hate to think of us being inside even if it is a beloved dwelling. The climate of Ireland is selfish as it relates to warmth and sunlight. Too long the rainy days and cold snows of winter. The Atlantic wind does not spare our watery Ireland. My county Sligo knows both the warmth of the summer sun and the wrath of the winter's gale."

"You must love Sligo. What about it attracts you so?" she asked.

"Besides being the summer home of my family, the ocean and mountains appeal to me. The rising swells along the beach have a language all their own. When I was very young, I became interested in 'The Cattle Raid of Cooley.' As you know, Queen Medb of Connacht is mentioned in that story. I can only imagine what she was like at the dawn of Irish history. A Neolithic queen with absolutely power over her subjects including her husbands. There is little doubt that some of her control came from her great beauty. Such beauty allows for the easy manipulation of men."

"I, too know of the many legends that tell of her desire to both control and possess her lovers," Lady Gregory added as she raised the helm of her dress in the crossing of a small stream.

"Wait, please take my hand. The stones are very slippery," William said as he stepped into the shallow stream, extending his hand to Augusta.

Despite his hand, Augusta managed to slip on the moss-covered rocks. Immediately she fell into deeper water. Though summer's warmth prevailed, the frigid cold of the stream was felt. Her many layers of clothing acting to absorb the water quickly even though she arose immediately from her partial submersion. She then waded to the shore; her linen skirt clinging closely to her body.

"Augusta! Augusta! Please forgive me for not being able to grab you more quickly. I was losing my own balance at the same time you were falling." After helping her climb the embankment, William sat down on a large protruding stone and emptied water from his shoes.

"Have no regrets, it was my stream into which I fell," Augusta whispered as she trembled under the shade of a great oak tree as water ran down her face and fell between her breasts. "The tower is not far from here, and the staff will have a nice fire waiting for us. We will be able to dry ourselves once we arrive."

As they walked, light, filtered by leaves, fell upon them as they hurried towards the castle known as Thoor Ballylee. Woodland birds accompanied them on their walk. Squirrels chased one another on the branches of the overhanging trees. Under their feet came the sounds of leaves, acorns and mulch.

Ascending to the well-traveled road, they crossed the stone bridge over Coole River. William stopped to observe the large trout waiting in the shade for the appearance of the mayflies. They appeared motionless except for the beating of their pectoral and pelvic fins.

"William, do not be so long staring at the trout. Your feet are very wet; just like my own. We must dry both your socks and your shoes," Augusta said gently as she motioned for him to join her.

With her wet clothes creating a cast-like image of her body, she appeared to be very small; even delicate. "You are right, Augusta, the trout can wait until we are dry."

Smoke and the scent of peat hung in the air until the wind once more moved the boughs of the trees. Dragonflies darted about the edges of the river as they pursued one another upon the currents of air. The yard had recently been sickled and, therefore, had the fresh smells of stacked hay and wild field onions; an unplanned banquet of scents greeted them though unintentionally invited.

Augusta turned the latch and pushed the heavy door of oak and steel bands. "How nice it is to be where there is warmth." The white stone walls of the first floor reflected both the light of the sun and of the flames within the hearth.

"I love the sound of running water and spitting hearth," William said as he bowed his forehead, upon entering the tower door, so as not to hit his head on the low threshold.

Augusta smiled. "I am glad you remembered how small the entryway is to a tower. It was, of course, one of the defensive strategies used. If the doorway was kept small, the defenders could spear invaders through the murder hole one at a time."

"Yes, I remember that from my readings," said William. "A perfect defense in an era before gunpowder."

Upon entering the room, they both walked to the fire and extended their hands towards its warmth.

"Augusta, I suggest you change into something warm. Then we will need to dry our wet clothing," William mentioned with some hesitation. He had no idea how his suggestion would be taken.

"William, I am afraid I do not have a complete change of clothing in the tower. I try not to leave such items here for fear they will become victims of mildew. Please turn your head while I remove my outer garments so that I can place them by the fire."

William turned away and looked towards the windows of the room. There upon the glass was a faint reflection of Lady Gregory beginning to undress. He watched as she undid the outer buttons of her dress which fell to the floor. He then turned further away from the vision within the window glass. He was a person ruled by desire and controlled by respect. He did not yet feel free enough to gaze upon such a beautiful person at such a potentially intimate moment where instinct must remain subservient to reason.

As he looked away she spoke, "William, you can turn around now. I have spread my outer garments and hose on the drying rack before the fire."

William turned to look at her. As she brushed, her black hair hung freely about her waist; her white chemise remaining damp.

"I will put more peat upon the fire," William offered.

"Please do, Thoor Ballylee has such a draft and my feet feel very cold."

"Augusta, if you will, you can put your feet on my lap to keep them warm," William offered.

"You make a kind offer, sir. I never anticipated such a need, but first, I want to put a kettle on the hearth rack and warm some water for tea. She walked to the table upon which had been placed a silver pitcher full of well water. He watched her thin fingers holding the copper kettle as she poured. Everything about her was harmonious. Her mannerisms, her physical appearance, her dedication to a task were all one.

"Lady Gregory, you make the pouring of water an art form."

"Thank you, William. You appear to appreciate the most simple of actions. This water comes from a nearby fairy well. Let us hope we have found favor with them."

As she stood at the table, her body highlighted before the window by the glow of sunlight, he admired her beautiful long black hair and the silhouette of her body. In her boldness, she showed strength in all circumstances.

"How does she know I can be trusted with her virtue?" he thought. "She is a woman of intellect yet strength."

❧13❧
The Fairy Ring

"Do you believe in the power of the fairies?" asked William.

"I have studied and recorded the mythology of Ireland in great detail. If you believe in them, then they exist," Augusta replied.

"You enchant me, Augusta."

"I must be careful or you will think me to be a fairy." Augusta laughed.

William returned her smile. "I remember a poem I read in my youth. I think the name of it was 'A Dance of Fairies About the Yew Tree.' He turned towards the window as he recited the verses from his childhood:

> *"The night sings in cricket and forest bird*
> *That upon the trees do cling.*
> *While phantoms dance*
> *The rim of a wheel in the darkened glade.*
>
> *"Not the English rowan tree do I seek,*
> *But that of which the clan does speak.*
>
> *"To sit in quietness beside the stream.*
> *Does not the fairy well provide the drink?*
>
> *"Can love be silent like the streaks of dawn?*

From mountain peak
"The colors do drift upon the trees.

"In a secret garden
Not yet arrayed in morning's color;
I await my love while fairies dance about the yew."

"William, I admire you for having remembered a poem from your childhood. I think that in every Irishman there is a desire to believe. Not far from the tower is a fairy ring. I remember walking alone one foggy morning. The sun has just arrived behind the winter limbs of a great oak. There in the center of the ring was a small person dancing. Her hair was as red as the leaves of fall and hung down in one long braid. Her white dress was covered in wild flowers that fell from it as she danced. She did not look my way while I stood enchanted. I could not hear any music yet her movements were those that indicated a lively dance was being performed. I stood in absolute amazement and did not venture near. I was afraid the young girl would hear the beating of my heart in both fear and amazement."

Augusta continued, "The sun then broke free of the limbs of the tree and light flooded the meadow and the ring. There was no one there. I called and called but no one but a raven answered me. I have often wondered what became of the young maiden. She was as beautiful as Saint Bridget."

William responded, "I understand that the rings appear whenever an elf or fairy queen is near. If one is drawn into the circle, that person will not be free to return from the grasp of the fairies. I heard a story about a young maiden that joined the dance within the ring. Her lover stood in amazement and looked upon her beauty, and the beauty of the maiden who had invited her to dance within the circle. Then her lover realized she was being taken by the fairy queen. Luckily for him, they had carried a honeycomb with them to eat during their picnic. He placed the comb in his ears to silence the music and, thereby, avoided the charm. He dashed into the ring and grabbed her hand. As he held her, she and the fairy disappeared. All that remained were a circle, not of stone, but of mushrooms dwelling in the grass."

"That is a beautiful, yet sad story. You know, William, that not all circles are as temporary as mushrooms. The circle I speak of is made of carefully placed stones. If we were not still wet, I would take you to see it. There is a great oak tree nearby which gives, I believe, a mystical power to the stones. I have been told that because of its great strength, fairies live among the branches. The Druids believed that if mistletoe grew upon the oak, then spirits lived within like souls that dwell within a cathedral. "

"Augusta, you have made me think of the magical trees among which we walked. If I remember the stories of peasants, the holly tree is used to remove the spell of witches. It was a sacred tree to our ancestors, the early Celts. Of additional interest to me is how the fairies have contributed not only to our culture but to the literary world. Our Irish puca was even honored by playing a part in Shakespeare's *Midsummer Nights' Dream*. Of course being English, he changed the name to Puck of which, I might add, I approve."

Augusta looked towards William. "Yes, I am familiar with Castle Pook located in Doneraile, County Cork; a long deserted ruin. I visited there as a small child. If I remember correctly, it was a summer picnic with my parents. It was a beautiful day; the fields about the castle were splendid in their covering of flowers; colors embroidered into summer's skirt.

"Nearby there is a large cave in which a good natured giant dwelled. He protected the nearby village and ground corn in the night to provide both food and income for the peasants. The peasants would leave their corn on their doorsteps and the giant would gather it. The next morning, freshly ground corn would be left. The giant did have one great dislike; he did not desire to be seen. One night a man filled with whiskey stayed up and saw the giant. In his rage, he stopped grinding the village corn. The only trace of him that remains is his cave and his name."

She continued, "Of course, as children, we entered the cave only to be frightened by a cousin's scream. I remember the warm embraces of both my mother and father. I loved their protecting nature."

A FAIRY WELL DEEP IN THE WOODS OF COUNTY GALWAY

"I must admit, Augusta, that I too have found many mysteries in Ireland. The fairy wells have always attracted me even though now they wear the name of Christian saints. I remember a well dedicated to Saint Daitlean. The water is very clear yet you cannot see the bottom. As in the past, protection is given by throwing a coin into the water. Some say it is a trick nurtured by the fairies to get visitors to give them gold."

"Did you toss a coin into the water?" she asked.

"Of course, probably not enough to merit their attention." William laughed.

"There is a well in County Galway deep in the forest that appears to be filled with debris. Yes, it is true that dead leaves and sticks of decaying wood float upon its waters. Yet, if you look closely, you will see patches of cloth that the peasants have cast into the well. From the cloth, the fairies weave their clothes with golden thread," added Augusta.

Augusta shook the top of her chemise. "I think I am getting dry. Would you like to walk to my fairy ring? Perhaps we will see the young girl dancing."

Both William and Augusta began to lace their shoes. The leather felt cold and moist upon their feet. Even though Augusta had discovered within the tower a dark blue coat that would have covered her form-fitting 'artistic dress,' she did not put it on; she remained in her ivory-white chemise. She covered only her shoulders in a woolen wrap that had been left behind in the tower.

Outside, the air was warm and very crisp. The winds from off the Atlantic brought sea smells to Coole Park. The river provided the musical bed to the melodies of the wild birds and gaily clad finches.

They paused once more upon the bridge; each silent in their own thoughts. William remembered words written to him by an English girlfriend with whom he had corresponded:

It is the fall of the year.
Color clings to trees like dabs of oil upon the artist's canvas.
Rocks obedient to the current that etches both stone and riverbank.

I look into your eyes and would dwell there much longer yet we of

Necessity must soon leave.
We have only a moment to pause as we listen to water played
by stone.
We see the river approaching from a spring that flows from a
mountain slope.
Downstream, the waters from smaller streams move more
peacefully as one.

I know we are impermanent as the water that, in melodious
choral
Sounds, reverberates beneath our feet.
Soon the river changes course and flows towards that not seen.

I speak of love and hold you close.
You will soon be taken from me as summer leaves in mixed
color fall.
I would that we would remain a thousand years upon this
bridge.
To hold so tight that we in frozen motion stay.

We, like this mountain river, journey towards that unknown.
Will it be to the ocean or an unnamed stream where calm
waters
Collect in pools etched in stone?

She turned towards him; their eyes meeting in a prolonged glance. They then walked towards the grove of trees that adjoined the fairy ring; tree leaves glistening in the sun. There beneath the great oak and formed into a perfect circle were the stones of the fairy ring. "I wish I had brought my paint so I would be able to capture such a sight."

William placed his hand on her shoulder as one might a friend. "I have often wondered what would happen to a man and a woman that made love within such a ring?"

Augusta did not answer nor did she remove his hand from her shoulder. The grass within the ring was a brilliant green and still moist from the early morning hours for the great oak had protected it from the sun until their arrival.

"William, I do not know of anyone brave enough to have done so. Would it amuse the fairies or challenge them to a prank or even worse, to capture the lovers' souls."

"Augusta, is it not the unknown that beckons us to creativity?"

"Surely you are not suggesting that we make love today. We hardly know one another. To make love is the most intimate of exchanges between a man and woman. At the moment of orgasm, they do not exist as individuals; all identity is lost. It is to play with emotions in a game we cannot control."

He removed his hand from her shoulder and took her hand in his own. He turned her towards him. Her eyes remained upon the ground until he placed his hand beneath her chin; a silent communication within a glance.

"William, I am attracted to you, that is a certainty. I don't know why I am so willing to lose all reasoning and pursue this matter of the heart. It cannot be love that I seek but the moment of love when all else ceases about me."

His hands began to unbutton her chemise.

❧14❧
The Bonding

William did not realize that having lain as one within the fairy ring, a bond greater than marriage would be formed; a bond that would last throughout their life not even ending with their deaths. It would now be impossible for them to love another; two lives to be lived separately yet never part.

They rested for more than an hour on the green grass within the fairy ring. It was difficult for William to remain awake for never in his life had he known such peace and restfulness as he did at that moment. The ambition and consequent conflicts of his life did not exist within the ring. He had entered, unknown to him, the cloister of a forest cathedral upon whose altar they had lain; having become themselves the sacrament.

Afterwards, Augusta entered the now warm waters of the turlough and stood there as the clouds were painted in differing colors by the afternoon's changing light. She gathered the bloom of a water lily and placed it in her hair as William watched enchanted. The wild flowers alongside the water moved with the ever-changing rhythm of the wind. Soon a shower of sparking raindrops baptized her in radiant light.

The light of the dimming sun poured forth its golden light upon the meadow and surrounding woods. William reached for her hand and held it lightly within his own. A full moon was rising through the trees and sat but for a moment upon the hills. The colors of the day would soon be fading and in their place, the soft face of the newly risen moon would appear as red as the embers within a flame.

She finished buttoning her chemise as they walked towards Thoor Ballylee. Augusta was the first to speak, "Will you stay with me this night? There is much that we can learn of one another."

William did not know how to respond, yet he yearned for her as for no other. He sensed the depth of expression within her that was not present in Maud Gonne. Maud Gonne's being revolved around her causes of land reform and Irish independence. There was no room in her heart for another; especially a man that did not carry the passion required to venture towards both unrest within his very soul and the self-destructive path of the warrior consumed by the flame of Irish independence.

"Will your staff not be worried that you have not returned to your estate house?" he asked.

"My staff knows that I often stay at the castle. When it becomes too late in the evening, it is safer for me to remain inside rather than wander about the woods and turloughs of Coole Park."

"Then, yes, I will stay with you," said William in a soft voice. "I doubt if Edward will notice that I have not returned to his estate. I have on more than one occasion mentioned to his coachman that if I am late, Coole Park will provide transportation for me.

Augusta looked into his eyes. "Promise me you will never mention this day to anyone. Not in your poems or any other writing. Promise me."

"This time never existed for either of us. But why should I deny such passion in my writings?"

"We are all aware that writers of verse wear the masks of their own identity. Your words will be but layers of transparencies. Do we not know the characters about whom Lord Byron wrote? Even the Scottish maid, May Gray, resides within our thoughts to this day," said Augusta.

"It is true we are the people we have loved. Would I now not be incomplete if I removed this day from my being?" William responded.

"You must," Augusta replied.

"Then let our love be known in a future time when those who would now complain are, like we must soon be, no more."

William pushed hard against the heavy door of the tower castle. The warmth of the day had not left the room. The flowers that Lady Gregory had gathered earlier and placed upon the table provided an aroma conducive to romantic thought. The sounds of the flowing river continued to enchant him as did her presence.

"William, what you must remember is that Sir Gregory has been dead but four years. In addition, I am much older than you. This society will not abide with that fact. Our culture admires a gentleman of years who takes a young wife, but the opposite is not true. It would greatly hurt the cause of Ireland if our affair ever became known. You must someday forget me and find another closer to your own age. A man with your traits will have no difficulty in finding a woman to fall in love with him. I will then remain your lover only in your thoughts."

"Find another what? Do you think that marriage and procreation is all that matters to me? Augusta, what have we to do with rules? Why should I care about those that would deny us pleasure, even if but momentary? We have seized the moment, and I have no regret."

"Nor I," responded Augusta.

The ivory-white chemise was once more removed from her shoulders as his hands traveled the texture of her skin.

The morning light too soon entered the room and touched their faces. As she lay in his arms, the sounds of the river and the squawking of wild ducks awakened them. As William lit the peat he had earlier placed in the fireplace, Augusta remained in bed admiring his tall, lean form.

"I would that we could always remain within this room," Augusta said sincerely. "I have never known such contentment as I know now."

"I, too feel that of which you speak. This moment belongs to us and no one else. Perhaps the Fairy Ring has bewitched us both."

William reentered the bed as Augusta held the blankets up in anticipation of his arrival. "I love you, William, if only for this moment."

He placed his arm across her turned side and then dwelt within her warmth.

Augusta spoke softly, "We must leave now though. I would prevent it if I could, but the staff will be concerned. I have never stayed so long away from the house when visiting the tower. You and I must not be seen after such a long period together. I am certain there will be talk regardless of what we do or say."

William answered, "I will walk towards Edward's estate. I believe there will be someone to give me a ride in their wagon along the road to Gort."

"I must see you again, it is the will of the Fairies and mine." Lady Gregory laughed as she combed her long, black hair. She then lowered her chemise from about her shoulders and said, "I will send word to you through Edward."

William stood in the entryway to the castle looking at her beauty. "What did I not see when I first saw her? She is far from plain. Her beauty grows within me for a reason I cannot comprehend; a flower awakened in the garden."

❧15❧
Party at Coole House

William was in Donegal when he received a telegram from Edward:

Party at Coole Park, March 15. Lady Gregory
continues to talk only of you. Must come! Edward.

William read the telegram over again. March 15, the Ides of March. "Augusta must have known that I would note the date and the significance of its meaning. Happiness, the loss of reason and madness all occur on that day. I, too know that a full moon is present and the sea will rise to strike the Cliffs of Moher. The fairies must be happy with anticipation."

The date that William received the telegram was March 14, 1897. From his window, he looked upon the rain that fell into the streets. Outside, the hoofs of horses struck loudly on the cobblestone. Earlier in the day, he had sat in the gardens of O'Donnell Castle to smell the flowers and to listen to the conversations of the Irish-speaking population. William had also managed to walk briefly along the shores of Lough Eske. He had hoped to enjoy fishing for the early spring salmon just before the heavy rains had spoiled the day. He was satisfied, however, for he did manage to have a most pleasant walk earlier in the nearby Ardnamona woods.

He rapidly packed his bags for the afternoon carriage ride to Coole Park. When the telegram arrived, he had started to compose a poem that would capture the moments of what had been a most splendid day. He now felt anguish in that he could not interpret the emotions that caused him to accept so quickly the invitation. He only knew that he must leave before the rising waters created a problem for his carriage.

Quickly he arrived at the entryway to the Abby Hotel where the carriages to Galway stopped to embark passengers for the trip to Galway. He felt most fortunate as the carriage arrived soon after his arrival in the lobby of the hotel.

Boarding the carriage, he was seated next to a most attractive young lady. Across from him sat a small-framed woman in the raiment of one who has recently mourned. She stared at him as the carriage began to move. "Dear sir, I assume you are traveling to Galway."

"Yes," responded William."

"To see a lover?" the older woman asked.

William was taken aback by the abrupt question. "Of what affair is it of hers?" he thought.

"Perhaps," he responded.

"Tomorrow is the Ides of March. Be careful with your heart, young man," she said as she glanced out the window of the carriage.

ঙ16ঙ
A Carriage of Strangers

The carriage took the coastal route to Galway. As it made its way along the rocky and occasionally treeless coast, views of the pounding sea could be seen as seagulls were lifted by strong gusts above the crashing swells of a distant Atlantic storm. The screams of petrels could be heard.

The young lady next to William remained silent. Occasionally she would smile at him when he turned to look out the window next to her. Outside, he could see the distant slopes of Benbulben.

"Young man, it will not be too long until we reach Drumcliff," said the older woman. "Are you familiar with this area?

"Yes, I am. My family often summers in County Sligo. While others may choose to sit, I prefer to journey to the small towns and rural areas," William acknowledged as the carriage bounced upon the stony outcroppings of Connemara.

"There is a fine view of Benbulben from the churchyard at Drumcliff," she added.

"Yes, I have passed by it several times. In fact, I have attended services there that were conducted by a relative."

"Sir, you must be a man of faith."

"I consider myself to be of such a persuasion," commented William.

She then looked towards the sun-touched slopes of Benbulben. "I too believe in that which cannot be seen so easily as one's outward faith."

"Madam, you intrigue me. You, by your very own statement, have implied that your faith dwells within you; how can such strength remain unseen? Can that which is not seen be brought forth?

"Yes, if properly summoned."

"Are you a medium of séances?

"Yes, I have just been at the home of a fine family just east of Donegal. They requested my visit."

"For what reason? To entertain the bored gentry?" Before she could respond, he continued, "I must also ask if the séance occurred at Lissadell House? If so, I know the family. I was a childhood friend of Countess Markievicz.

"No, it was not Lissadell House, nor was I there to entertain the bored gentry. I was invited to a different nearby estate to communicate with the master's lost daughter. She vanished while searching for shells along the coast."

"What was the result of your quest? Where they satisfied?"

"Oh yes, indeed, they paid me fifty pounds."

"That is a generous amount," commented William.

"Not only can I communicate with the spirit world, I am a teller of the future."

"That is interesting. What do you see in my future besides the romance you described? Will I be well known and successful in business?

"Sir, I cannot answer such questions for you have not yet paid me," she replied.

William looked at the white-capped waves and the sparking of the sun upon the distant slate sea, "Would you be free to entertain us at Lady Gregory's estate at Coole Park? Her estate is just outside Gort. I don't think she is the kind to object to such a visit. It should prove very entertaining. If the fee she offers is not satisfactory, I will be willing to pay for your carriage ride back to Galway."

"Only if my daughter's friend can accompany us," she said.

"Who is her friend?"

"The young lady seated next to you, of course."

He looked towards the young woman whose beauty had not gone unnoticed. "My name is William."

Silenced ensued. "I know," the beautiful stranger dressed in yellow replied.

"Have we met before?" William asked having become uncomfortable with her brief reply.

"My name is Olivia Shakespear. I am sure you have never heard of me."

"Olivia Shakespear. No, I don't recognize that name. Should I?"

"I am of no consequence to you. "

"How could that be? We share the same coach and your friend's mother has invited you to the party I am also attending."

"You are a dramatist, a poet and a scholar. I am nothing but a female riding in a coach with you."

"Please do not be critical of your sex. Many of my friends possess both beauty and intellect. Your sex is the missing part of any man's happiness. We cannot be complete without you. From your expressions, you are a well-educated lady of good breeding."

"Sir, your comment reduces me to that of livestock."

"I apologize," said William with surprise.

"I am neither well-educated nor of landed birth. I am a writer, that is true, but have sold very little of my talents. I also have written two plays that did not receive favorable reviews."

"Of what do you write? I take it you are interested in the occult since you must have just attended a séance," William asked.

"Yes, that is true," she responded. "Who is not interested in knowing the answer to the greatest question we all have. I will answer your inquiry, though my answer will only serve to disappoint. My great interest is in the interplay between man and woman; in other words, affairs of the heart."

"You have taken on a most difficult and controversial subject. What have you learned that you might share with me?"

"I have learned that men do not lead, but are followers. They are ruled not by reason but by the most basic of instinct. A woman, when truly loved, is in total control. She tends to play him as a fisherman does a trout in the River Corrib. She allows him to race from her only to tantalize him and then she pulls him back." As Olivia spoke, she acted out the role of a fisherman pretending to reel a lively fish.

William enjoyed the dramatization before him as did the older woman. "Olivia from your performance, you belong on the stage. Perhaps I shall write you into one of my plays." Then he smiled. "See, I did not misjudge your character. You are well read and a most genuine tribute to your sex."

Olivia returned his smile. "Yes, that is true. I am a lover of literature."

"I noticed by your ungloved hand, that you are married."

"I am indeed, sir. I also have a daughter named Dorothy."

"I am afraid that is something we do not have in common. I do not have a wife. I would that I could find someone to love. I think also that I would also be a very good father."

"By the use of the word 'find,' you imply that locating a mate is a search; something to do, like looking for your trousers in the morning."

William felt he had met his equal. He did not know how to respond to such a remark. Was she now a fisherman? Was she about to set a hook in his mouth only to play him like the trout in the river?

At his silence, she smiled and looked out the carriage window as they crossed the stone bridge in Sligo City. "What is that tall mountain rising about the city?" she asked. "It appears to have a monolith upon its top that resembles a young boy's paddy cap."

"It is Medb's cairn that you see on the top of Knocknarea. I have climbed to the cairn many times. The first time that I climbed Knocknarea, I managed to fall in front of a young lady. She found it difficult to control her laughter. Since then, I have always climbed it alone."

"You prefer that your mistakes are hidden from others?" she asked.

William continued, ignoring her question, "I must warn you that if you ever climb the mountain, you must carry a stone with you to place upon the cairn or you will bring Medb's wrath upon you. Old people say she was buried standing upright facing her enemies just as she had appeared while living. One did not oppose her in life nor should a visitor oppose her now in death."

"How do you know so much about her?"

"I remember reading of her exploits in the *Táin* when I was very young. As you know, in ancient Ireland, women often ruled over men, and it was through their lineage that land and title passed. See, your sex is a bold strong one indeed. Have you not also read of Grace O'Malley whose raiding ships sailed along our coasts?"

"William, you are a very nice person. Your compliments and concern are quite touching as is your knowledge of our country," Olivia replied.

"Then Olivia, it is settled. You must accompany your friend's mother to Lady Gregory's. I know she will enjoy meeting a follow writer. If Lady Gregory permits your friend to conduct a séance, then you must participate as well." William then added, "I hope you both will be my guests for the evening. While Galway has many fine hotels such as the Hotel Meyrick, we have the opportunity to stay at a most glorious estate that is adjacent to the coast."

The older woman, Mrs. O'Malley, spoke first, "Sir, you have made us a most generous offer, but, as you know, we do not really know you, and I am certain Olivia would find it uncomfortable for us to stay at the home of a gentleman we have just met despite the merits of his offer."

"Let me assure you it is not my home but that of a friend's. I understand your concern, but obviously, my literary reputation has proceeded me for your daughter's friend has read of me. I would not risk my own reputation and that of my family to be less than the gentleman you expect me to be."

Olivia looked towards him with a coquettish smile. "William, I trust you to not tarnish both our reputations."

The carriage arrived at the Renvyle House in the early evening. Renvyle was a sea-gray stone house in Connemara that belonged to Oliver St. John Gogarty. Lady Gregory had arranged for William to spend the night there on his way to Coole Park. Since Oliver was not present and the house was still staffed, William thought it not to be an inconvenience if his fellow guests also were accommodated.

The coach driver agreed to take them to the house carriageway, stating he would send someone from Galway to pick them up in the morning so that the journey to Coole Park could continue.

They soon found themselves standing before a six-bay, three-story house with age-darkened slate roof. The upper floor, with its narrow windows, provided accommodations for the numerous servants required to maintain such a home.

"Sir, may I take the ladies' trunks and yours? My name is Phillip, a member of the staff."

"Yes, please do," William answered.

The two ladies and William stood motionless in front of the house. Seagulls flew near them as though expecting a morsel to be thrown into the air. The sounds of the surf hitting the rocks on the nearby shore could be heard. A moon veiled in lace was seen rising near the Twelve Bens.

William and Olivia exchanged glances as they walked up the steps to the entryway. "Olivia, I like the fact that you are a 'chancer.' That is not a common characteristic among my acquaintances."

Olivia smiled. "Aren't you one also?"

As they entered the portico, and then walked into the great hall, a sea chill greeted them. "Phillip, would you mind lighting the fires. I am sure Oliver would not object." Soon the house was to feel traces of heat as peat, coal and wood fires provided their comforting warmth.

From his sea-facing windows, William looked at the darkening ocean upon which kelp floated among the collecting spume. Upon the sea, the setting sun could be seen spilling through the sails of a coastal schooner.

Olivia also stood before her window looking at the breakers whose sound penetrated her room. She could not help but think about the tall, dark-haired stranger she had only read about. His tweed suit and horn-rimmed glasses seemed to her a scholarly uniform if not an attraction to her desire.

William began to be concerned that his impromptu invitation might appear awkward upon their arrival at Coole Park. It would be easy enough to explain his invitation to Mrs. O'Malley, but his growing relationship with Olivia might not be so well received. In his thoughts, he searched for the obvious answer to the spontaneity of his decision, his compulsive desire to manifest his attractiveness to women.

Within two hours of their arrival, a knock was heard upon his door. "Sir, it is Phillip; dinner will be served in half an hour."

The dining room had large windows that looked seaward. The dark-wood beamed ceiling added to the ship like feel of the large room. At one end was a fireplace with its marble mantel. Lighted candles glowed from the mahogany table. Ornate napkin rings and fine silver had been placed at each seating.

There upon the table were brown trout and salmon fresh from the waters of the estate. Fresh oysters rested aboard their shells. The rich smell of many varieties of breads added a most pleasant aroma to the room. Fresh cooked vegetables provided color to the potpourri of foods. William arose as Olivia and Mrs. O'Malley entered the room.

Phillip had placed William at the head of the table and both ladies to either side.

William looked towards Olivia. "I am very pleased with my room. I hope your accommodations are as pleasant. Did you find anything in your room to read?"

Olivia responded, "Yes, I did. I now must make a difficult choice. Near my bed had been placed Thomas Hardy's *Tess of the d'Urbervilles*, George Eliot's *Middlemarch* and Charlotte Brontë's *Jane Eyre*. Being of a literary persuasion, what would you recommend?"

"Seeing that you have found yourself in a large house with a man you truly do not know, I suggest you read *Jane Eyre*."

"Am I to find myself also a character in the plot?"

"What a fascinating question to ask. What possible comparisons could be made? Perhaps you will let me know when you have read the story," he responded.

Olivia then appeared more serious. "This is a landed estate just as Thornfield Hall was. Mr. Rochester was a stranger to Jane just as you are to me. Jane had few choices and was the victim of her circumstance when she arrived at Thornfield. In my life, I too am a victim of low social status, and I found myself unable to resist your kind offer despite my own misgivings."

"Olivia, Jane Eyre felt a clash between her passion for god and her desire for Rochester. I doubt if such a conflict exists between us."

"William, you are correct. I shall remember to protect my heart from errant desires regardless of the attraction felt," she said with a radiant smile.

"We must always be careful we are not consumed by fire." William had allowed his leg to rest against Olivia's knee as they spoke, and she in return, through her inaction, had granted him permission. The physical contact with her felt reassuring. He wondered if she would readjust her chair so as to move further away from him. Yet, she did not.

Ms. O'Malley had followed their conversation with great interest being careful not to interject her own opinion into the discussion. "William, would you be so kind as to pass the wine decanter to me? I believe this to be an excellent vintage, one that I cannot afford at home." No other words were spoken until the completion of the meal.

"Olivia, would you enjoy a walk along the shore? The sun is now reaching the horizon of the sea and will soon be gone. I think it wrong to return to our rooms in silence when a lively discussion might yet ensue."

She took his arm and together they walked down the stone steps and followed a narrow path to the sea. "William, I am going to take off my shoes so I can feel the warm sand yet soon to be cold; I fear there is no warmth in the sea."

With her words, William pressed her body to his as though offering warmth. He then removed his own shoes and stockings. She released his arm and took his hand and placed it in her own.

William pointed towards the ocean. "You see that large schooner that now appears only on the horizon. Earlier it had captured the sun within its sails; they then yielded a brilliant red glow. We must be careful the light does not pass too swiftly before us." William paused. "Earlier you did not move when our legs touched and now you have taken my hand. Boldness is a virtue you possess."

Olivia did not respond but continued to look down the beach where the fog had entered the narrow strait. William spoke once more, "You are married and have a child while I am single. Should I pursue you knowing there can be no resolution to any desire that arises beyond tomorrow's sunrise?"

"The roles we are assigned are written only in books and not in our hearts. I am made both strong and weak by my nature," she replied.

"I will be honest with you. I invited you earlier for a most curious of reasons. I am in love with Augusta Gregory. She has assured my agony in her refusal of my open pursuit. She has placed her own interest above my own. By having you, a beautiful young lady, in my presence, I had hoped to return the discontent she has cast upon me perhaps unintentionally."

William stopped walking and turned towards Olivia. "I have no role now to play."

"Will you come to my room tonight?" asked Olivia knowing that no mere mortal man could refuse such an offer.

"You create the greatest conflict within me. I have just confessed my love for Augusta and yet you invite me to forsake my fidelity to her. How can I say no to your request and deny my own longings, yet what I seek is more enduring. You are married and have a child. What possible future could there be for us except one that brings sorrow to both?"

Olivia looked towards him. "For what future do you live? Do you not know that we do not live in the past or in the future? I have asked not for your heart but for you to share my bed."

"Can we draw so near and not be burned?" William said as the strong sea wind blew his long black hair. They were both standing in the water having not observed the rising tide that now undulated about their feet; their faces moistened by the breath of the nearing wind-tossed waves.

William looked once more at her. "When we have fled from this beach, what will remain of us? Even our footsteps are now being removed by the sea and wind. Look, the tide is rising and yet we have not moved. Your words have held me here like the anchor cable of our thoughts."

Olivia looked steadfastly into his eyes. "Then lie with me and cover me with your words."

William was absorbed in a great conflict he had designed himself; not to lie with Olivia, but to convince Augusta of her need for him.

He took her hand and did not speak. Slowly they walked back to Renvyle House. The wind was blowing even stronger; bending the limbs of both shrubs and trees. The red fuchsia, like Chinese paper lanterns, moved to the beat of the ocean's wind.

"I will wait for you," Olivia said as he released her hand.

William remained silent as he watched her walk up the large, opulent stone staircase. On the first landing, she turned around, stood still for a moment and smiled at him. She knew he had not removed his stare from her as she ascended.

William walked about the great house stopping in the billiard room where decanters of various whiskeys demanded attention. Wood fire cast differing colored lights upon the crystal glass as he held it to pour from the decanter. The fire spoke through cracking and popping sounds. He sat down in a velvet-lined chair by the fire, feeling the heat upon his head and uncovered hands.

Why, when he desired nothing more than to find peace, had such a conflict of intent been so cast upon him? Was he no more than the beasts that roam Coole Park under the fullness of the moon? Yet he longed for Olivia, her beauty and boldness. Had their meeting been preordained by some goddess who desired such sport for her amusement?

He looked towards the door of the billiard room. From there, he could see the great staircase that led to the bedchambers of the house. "Once done, it cannot be undone," he thought.

He raised himself from the fireside chair and began to walk down the open hall towards that to which no repentance ever truly removes the sin from conscious thought; no prayers said often enough to mend the heart; yet he walked, powerless, insect-like towards the flame.

William stood before the large, oaken door. He knocked lightly on its surface. With soft tones he spoke, "Olivia, Olivia." Other rooms were nearby and he desired not to disturb Mrs. O'Malley or the staff. In the Georgian homes, with their wide-planked wooden flooring, sounds carried great distances especially during the night when guests, owner and staff listened for sounds that might indicate the presence of an intruder or the restlessness of a troubled spirit.

"Olivia, Olivia," he spoke again. She did not respond to his inquiry. Slowly he turned the knob. The door protested on its hinges as he entered. Beyond lay the open window; lightweight drapes moving to the undulating wind. Moonlight covered the trees with silver within the yard and sparkled upon the sea. The only inhabitants of the room were silhouettes.

"William, I am standing here," she said. He turned to see her outline in the dimness of the room. She moved towards the moonlit window and paused. Her hair had not been let down yet she was dressed in a sleeping gown of sheer material through which moonlight revealed her form. "You came to me just as I predicted. I now control you as the moon does the sea."

"Pray for me," he said out loud. A request to which she did not respond. She waited as a silhouette within the room.

At first, he hesitated, unsure of his intentions. Then he moved towards her, embracing her passionately as the drapes moved about their shoulders. Her chemise fell to the oaken floor. His hands grasped her as a priest might the soul of a parishioner.

❧17❧
Arriving

Upon reaching Galway, the carriage stopped at the King's Head Inn for refreshment, potential passengers and mail. As the guests entered the pub, they noticed the date "1612" cut upon the stone fireplace. The King's Head Inn was considered one of the landmarks of Galway. The eight-hundred-year-old pub's evolving architecture was built upon its 13th century foundation.

The name came from one of the owners having been the executioner of Charles I on 3 January 1649. Quite possibly the executioner also exported white slaves to work his plantation in the West Indies.

"Olivia, will you allow me to buy you a pint?" asked William who had avoided additional conversation in the carriage. He felt that silence would distance him from last night's affair.

Olivia replied, "Only if you will talk with me while we drink. I feel that conversation will aid us in making the trip seem shorter. I think you will make an interesting character in one of my books. You are aloof, passionate and gifted; the perfect character for a gothic novel. What do you think?"

Suddenly, William felt the same concerns that Augusta had expressed to him at their departure from Thoor Ballylee. "I would very much appreciate it if you would forget about last night and, certainly, not write about it. Even though we may pretend that our plots and characters are fictional, we both know they are not. It always amazes me how easily critics can determine the truth of our words."

"Well said, poet. The remaining question for me is whether I should obey your desire or fulfill my own. Can a writer be silent when words flow so easily?"

William replied, "I think it is unbecoming of a friend to deny a sincere request."

"Really, by whose rules must we live? I have already broken many covenants." Olivia smiled as she spoke.

William looked at the frothy head of the Guinness as bubbles rose to the top of his glass. He then looked at her unable to resist noting her remarkable beauty. The blue of her eyes and the fall-brown color of her hair. Her full lips red as though perpetually wine stained. "While you are truly beautiful, you do not have the heart of an Irish woman."

"Well said, as you know, I am not Irish but English. Perhaps neither my country nor my youth prepared me for compassion. My husband's occupation is one without pity when he appears before the bar. Your own personality is more like my step-niece's."

"Who might she be? Am I acquainted with her?" asked William.

"Perhaps you have not met her. Her name is Georgie Hyde-Lees. She and my daughter, Dorothy, are best friends."

"Are you inferring that I have the personality of a child?"

"Yes, I think you do. You want to explore like a child, but do not want to bear the responsibility for your actions. You are hesitant without cause."

"I think you have drunk your pint too quickly. The carriage is waiting for us," William said as he arose to follow Olivia into the bright light of High Street, a street alive with the sound of vendors and musical instruments played by those who performed for the sixpence of passing strangers.

The Carriage followed the road to Gort and then to Coole Park. As it entered the gates, William felt as though he were returning home. The familiar trees and turloughs; the walks he and Augusta had shared in the warm sun of summer.

Soon the carriage arrived at Coole House. Its walls of moss and ivy-covered stone seemed welcoming as they were greeted by the familiar and loyal staff. Additional servants from the house assisted in unloading the trunks.

"Sir, I was not aware we were having additional guests," said the doorman.

"I trust that Lady Gregory will not object to meeting two very fascinating people who share a common interest with her," replied William.

"What interest are you referring to?" Lady Gregory smiled. She had heard the conversation involving the two unknown visitors.

"Lady Gregory, I was not aware of your presence. It is my honor to present Mrs. O'Malley and her daughter's friend, Mrs. Olivia Shakespear."

"It is an honor having you at Coole Park. It is a pleasure to meet you both. William tends to have the most interesting and learned friends," Augusta said as she observed the clothing of each woman. She had earlier remarked to him that she could judge the profession, education and character of a person by how they dressed. Augusta placed more value upon the evaluation of apparel than she did in the ritual of formal greetings.

She noted immediately the flamboyant yet inexpensive clothing of Mrs. O'Malley. She immediately felt the presence of someone spiritual. Her judgment of

Olivia was quite different. The tightly corseted waist; the high-necked blouse stiffened with bone; her tightly woven hair covered by a fine hat reflecting the latest of Parisian fashion. Hers was that of an aesthetic style indicating a great love for the arts.

☙ 18 ☙
The Drawing Room

Augusta looked towards William expecting him to explain his invitation to the two contrasting ladies. William felt awkward as he observed her quizzical expression. "Mrs. O'Malley is a well-known medium. She just conducted a séance at the County Donegal estate of Baron and Lady Winslow."

William continued, "Mrs. Shakespear is a lover of literature, an author of novels as well as a playwright. She is a friend of Mrs. O'Malley's daughter and has offered to accompany Mrs. O'Malley to gain some materials for a new novel she plans to write."

Augusta looked towards her guest. "Mrs. Shakespear, my late husband, Sir Gregory, had spoken well of your husband," Augusta said while looking into the eyes of William as though questioning his intent to bring Olivia to Coole Park. She knew inwardly that William was attracted by Olivia's youthful beauty.

"I will direct my staff to place your trunks in the upstairs bedchambers. Please do join us later in my study. I imagine that you will then be ready for tea and biscuits," said Augusta to her awaiting audience.

Mrs. O'Malley responded, "Lady Gregory, that is very kind of you. Yes, tea will be very much appreciated. I understand that you will be conducting a séance this evening. Who will be conducting it?"

"Mrs. O'Malley, your arrival is most fortuitous. I received word just before your arrival that Mrs. Madelyn Smith, a dear friend of mine, is unable to conduct the séance. Her husband is ill. I had thought I would have to postpone the séance, that is, until you arrived. Will you be able to serve as our medium?"

"Yes, if it pleases you," said Mrs. O'Malley.

"Wonderful, then it is settled. We will all meet in the drawing room at 5:30 for tea."

As the guests were led to their rooms by the staff, Augusta said in a commanding tone, "William, will you speak with me for a moment?"

"Certainly, Augusta," replied William as he followed her into the Victorian room where light from the glass ceiling illuminated the many varieties of orchids and other flowers she had collected in her frequent walks around Coole Park.

Augusta spoke with a voice filled with anxiety. "Please, tell me why you invited two strangers to my house? That is not like you. You are too reserved to have taken such a bold action, however innocent it might be."

"I felt that you would enjoy meeting Mrs. O'Malley. Mrs. Shakespear had to accompany her since they are traveling companions."

"Are you sure that is all? I could not help but notice how you looked at Olivia," said Augusta, raising her voice as though she did not object to others hearing her reprimand.

"Why would you question my sincerity? I can assure you I care only for you," William said in a voice that revealed emotions fueled by both guilt and surprise at her blunt insinuation.

"William, have you confused love with physical desire?" Augusta sighed while maintaining eye contact.

"I do not understand what you mean. Trust is essential to love," William responded. As he spoke, it was apparent that moisture was forming on his forehead.

"I agree, but only a fool could deny her beauty. Please be careful, William, with both my heart and hers."

Tea and biscuits were promptly served at half-past five in the library. Upon entering the room, Mrs. O'Malley and Olivia heard the cracking of the wood that burn brightly in the fireplace. Behind them walked William who had been standing on the front porch looking at the swans in the nearby lake. He continued to be shocked at how quickly Augusta had judged him so accurately.

Augusta had seated herself in a red velvet fireside chair and was staring into the flames. The heat of the fire had earlier reminded her of Wilfrid and their passionate nights in Egypt. The smell of his cigar; the first night they embraced on the wide veranda of the house. The myriad sweet odors of the garden and his hands on her body as the wind from the Nile moved the drapes within the moonlit room.

William spoke, "Augusta, are we too early for tea?" He had noticed her intense concentration while looking at the flaming logs. It was most obvious to everyone that she had not sensed their presence upon entering the room. She then arose to address them as they too looked upon the fire.

"I have a great treat for all of us. Mr. John Synge will be joining us for the séance. I just had a telegram delivered to me. It seems he is visiting his uncle in Galway and asked if he might visit Coole Park. The moment I told him, William, that you were here, he insisted in having an opportunity to visit with you," Augusta said as she looked towards Olivia.

"Excellent," William replied. "I don't know if you ladies are acquainted with Mr. Synge. He is a man of many talents. If I didn't admire him so much, I would be jealous of him. Few men are as gifted as he is. Of great interest to John are the lives of the common people of Ireland. I think that is why I admire him so much. In literature, the common is largely ignored for the theatrical. With the passage of years, however, the common tends to become the exotic as literature provides the only view into that which is removed from us by time and with the consequent cloaking of events."

"Well said, William." Augusta replied. "You see, ladies, William and I, and a few others such as Mr. Synge, find the peasants of Ireland most deserving of our literary talents if we possess any. They are the most pragmatic of all people especially in their reactions to adversity. I used to think that John Synge was only interested in natural history especially noting the attention he paid to the birds of Coole Park, but I think his love of ornithology is what attracted him to my estate. We have so many turloughs that attract a wide variety of birds from all across Ireland."

"How can a poet ignore the swans of your many lakes? It is not the birds mounted in a study that create desire within the heart, but the natural environment they share. It is life that we who write celebrate," said William in a quiet voice.

Augusta shared a smile with William; their eyes looking into each other's soul for a prolonged period of time. "Yes, let me pour your tea," she said. The guests were honored that she was willing to serve them rather than asking a member of her staff, who waited patiently by, for a request.

The velvet seats in the room wore vivid colors; bright reds, oranges and blues yet the room was harmonious in its visual appeal. The dark-stained mahogany wood served like the frames of paintings; providing an excellent contrast to the bright colors of the chairs.

"I don't know if you know it or not, William, but John is very musically talented. We must ask him to play the piano," said Augusta.

"Ladies," William offered, "I hope that my friend does not offend you. Even though brought up in a religious family, Mr. Synge has lost his belief in God. He has found his faith to be incompatible with Church doctrine."

Olivia looked towards William. "Tell us about your faith. What inspires you?"

"I look for faith in what I see and express it in how I feel," he replied.

"Sir, you have given me the vaguest of answers. Help me to classify you. Are you an atheist, an agnostic or a spiritual person?"

"I am, that I am," he replied with a smile.

Olivia laughed. "You are no more a god than I am a goddess. Your faith is written on the sands of Donegal." William grasped the meaning of the two edges of her sword.

Augusta did not enjoy the exchange between the two. "I disagree with both of you. We are both god and mortal; conceited and humble."

William noted the emotional context within which Augusta spoke. "I apologize for my irreverent response. I take no pleasure in displeasing you, Augusta."

Just as he spoke, John Synge entered the room. Everyone became silent for they did not expect him so early in the evening. "Good evening, my friends. I know I have arrived earlier than expected but I could not resist joining you at the earliest possible moment. Your countryside is far more pleasant than either Galway or Dublin. I feel I have been too long away from the seven woods of Coole."

"You are most welcome to join us, John," said Augusta as she offered her hand to him. You are always welcome at our fireside. I understand that William convinced you to visit the Aran Islands. You must tell us about your experience there."

William interjected, "John, I feel guilty in suggesting such a journey considering that I understand you have not been feeling well of late."

"Just a problem with my glands. Nothing I cannot live with or eventually die from."

Olivia did not know how to take John's comment. "Sir, I have often wanted to go to the Aran Islands, but now you make me concerned about pestilence."

"Olivia, I am sorry. I should have explained. Recently, my glands became swollen, especially in my neck. It is just in my constitution. There is nothing to be concerned about. I must add that I never felt better in my life than I did on Inis Meáin."

"Thank you for clarifying that," said Olivia. "Why on earth would William encourage you to go to those barren, windswept islands whose inhabitants are the most primitive in Ireland? If I were to go to there, I would want my friends to pray both for my physical safety and sanity."

"I accept that your question and comment comes from an ignorance of those most beautiful sea-swept islands whose people are the apostles to both land and sea," replied John. "I am humbled by their unpretentious presence. I have learned how to face both life and death from them. Transformation is what occurs when we are confronted with a life-threatening illness that neither I, nor my doctors, understand. I can only trust that when I return there next summer, that they will once again provide me with solace."

Uneasy with the direction of the conversation, William intervened, "John, I am sure you would like to freshen up and then join us for tea."

"William, yes, my trip has not been an easy one. We have much to discuss later."

William noticed how tired John appeared to be as he paused on the staircase to rest before reaching the second landing. He had always appeared to be weakly even as a young person, being prone to infections; his health did not improve with age. It was very apparent that he was labored in his breathing.

Shortly, John returned to the drawing room apparently feeling much better. "You see, it just takes a moment and my health is restored," he said as he established eye contract with Olivia apparently hoping to improve their relationship.

"John, welcome back to the flock that is in desperate need of a shepherd," voiced Augusta.

Olivia added, "Lady Gregory earlier stated that you were a very accomplished musician. Would you do us the honor of playing something modern?"

"Recently, while I was in Paris, I had the honor of hearing Frederic Chopin play. I shall, with Augusta's approval, perform his Waltz in B minor, Opus 69.

As he played the hauntingly poetic composition, William's eyes met Augusta's. She stood next to John in order to turn the music while he played on her newly imported Baldwin grand piano. There was something in the music and the softness of the light upon her face and hair that intoxicated him. His betrayal of her the night before seemed incomprehensible, as though an entrapment had been accomplished.

As John finished, all members in attendance applauded him in recognition of his performance. William handed him a Scotch and water. "John, I have been intending to ask you about Cherrie Matheson. Has she finally accepted your marriage proposal?"

"William, I must confess I have now been rejected twice by her."

"She was an American, if I remember from our previous conversation about her," stated William.

"Yes, that is correct. She did not care for my lack of religious fervor. But I did want to thank you for encouraging me to go to the Aran Islands. My time there has inspired me to write once more."

"I hope to convince you to write full time. You are very original. I don't think I can find another friend like you."

William continued after pausing, "You have a gift for observing honesty in others; a rare gift indeed."

Having encouraged William to move to the far side of the room, John said with a serious tone, "Is she your friend or lover?"

"Who do you mean?" William appeared to be confused by such a blunt question.

"Who do you think that I mean? Surely you did not think I was speaking of Augusta, she is much too old for you."

"Oh, you are talking about Olivia. I must, however, address your comment related to my good friend, Augusta. Youth is an illusion. Does not all matter come from the dust of stars? We are all the same age regardless of the calendar. It is not the skin that attracts me to another but the intelligence within. Are not the works of Michelangelo of even greater value now that we have had time to understand and appreciate their meaning?"

"William, that is what distinguishes us one from another. I am a pragmatist that desires to write about reality. You are a dreamer; an impressionist in words. You still have not answered my question."

"Let's see, you asked me if she was my friend or lover. I think you have boldly asked me if Olivia and I have made love. My answer to you is 'yes' within the realm of verse."

"William, there you have once more answered, not with a clear response as I would have made, but more like a composer of riddles."

"Do you not think that a riddle is of more profit to a gossiper? An answer that stirs the imagination lends itself to greater detail than would one of objective fact. Your question implies you are interested in knowing Olivia better. Be careful my friend, the hourglass upon the belly of the Black Widow is clearly marked."

∿19∿
Visions

"Gentlemen and ladies, dinner is now served," a staff member called from the drawing room door as a small bell sounded. Each guest followed Augusta to the large dining room. There, about the 1810 George IV mahogany dining table, were eighteen chairs with splendid red velvet seats. Below the top of the table was a flamed mahogany frieze with beading below and a set of twelve legs turned at the top with tulip carving below, finishing on brass tipped castors.

Highly polished silver place sets adorned the table while four sets of candleholders paraded on the tabletop. A large baked ham had been prepared as well as a variety of wild game freshly killed by the gamekeeper. In addition, fresh salmon lay on sterling silver plates. The guests were offered their choice from a variety of red and white wines. Augusta had seated herself at the head of the table with William to her right and Olivia to her left. John had seated himself next to Olivia while Mrs. O'Malley set next to William.

The contrast between the two women could not have been greater. The classic beauty of Augusta and the sensuous beauty of Olivia were noticed by both men in the candlelight. While Coole Park had recently received its own generator for electric lights, Augusta preferred the soft light of candles and flaming logs; shadows moving freely upon the walls; playing with the great plaster medallions through which large crystal chandeliers were suspended.

"Olivia, William tells me you are gathering material for a novel that you hope to write. Please tell me about it," John requested.

"Lady Gregory, William is too ambitious for me. As you may know, a woman author is still handicapped by her sex."

Augusta replied, "Olivia, you must not make excuses. Jane Austin and Charlotte Brontë have shown that isn't an issue. What sustains an audience is the good telling of a tale. We are all captivated by that which has merit regardless of the author. When we are absorbed in the story, the writer vanishes, and we are left alone with the characters that now dwell within our imaginations. Do you think of the composer when music is played?"

"Have you a plot?" inquired Augusta so that William was able to hear her.

"Yes, I do but I do not want to bore you and your guests with such trivia."

"My dear, without your story, we will indeed be bored. How can the cooked flesh of a forest boar or a prepared wild salmon entertain us?"

John, who was listening intently to the conversation, could not help but laugh aloud. He, like William, realized that two brilliant and creative women were now engaged in a verbal joust, a contest of equals performed for the amusement of the court.

It was apparent to John that the contest must center around a man whose presence they both desired but could not share. "It could not be possible," he thought "that both Augusta and Olivia were lovers of the same man."

❧ 20 ❧
From the Other Side

The large adjoining parlor, to which the guests retreated after the meal, was cave-like in appearance due to the arched ceiling and dark paneling. Two large chandeliers hung from the ceiling that was adorned with oak beams cut from the forest of Coole Park.

Chairs were arranged around a carved round table made of exotic wood. Candles glowed with soft light mixed with bursts of color from the fire. The shadows of the room remained dark as though spirits dwelt within them. A large clock pronounced the time and monitored the flow of minutes. It was a room filled with people yet a sense of isolation reigned within.

Mrs. O'Malley appropriately waited for Augusta to seat the guests. Augusta indicated everyone to take their place around the table. Mrs. O'Malley was the last to be seated at the head of the table.

All waited for Augusta to speak. "Thank you for being here tonight. It is a true honor having such refined and published guests. Each one of you has contributed to the culture of Ireland in your own unique way." It was apparent that Augusta looked on Mrs. O'Malley as being of no higher status than one of her staff members.

Augusta continued, "Now I think it only appropriate to decide on the subject for tonight's séance. I must exclude, however, John from being able to offer a subject since he has no faith except that which can be proven objectively through scientific evidence. He peers at his god through a microscope." Uncomfortable laughter followed her comment.

She looked towards John. "Now that I have classified you as a nonbeliever, you may defend yourself if you wish to offer a subject for our amusement."

"Augusta, how can I respond to your words? When I said that I have no faith, I did not mean I lacked faith in science."

"Let me ask you a question. How can you be certain there is no god? He might be standing in one of the shadows in this room. It is impossible for you to view everything simultaneously, therefore, how can you be so sure of your convictions?"

"You want me to admit to being an agnostic; perhaps that is a truer statement of my condition. I can no more argue against you than I can argue for you. You have already won by casting doubt over my convictions. You see, I am like water. I take the form that resistance offers me." Those present felt he had admitted Augusta's strength of argument only through his desire to be congenial to a woman he greatly admired, and to whom he knew, could play a major role in his quest for literary fame.

Olivia looked towards John. "Now tell me who the weaker sex is?" She immediately laughed at the discomfort displayed in John by her comment. "Your convictions are destroyed by a nonsensical illustration."

John looked at her and did not respond. Even though he disliked her strength, he was possessed by her flirtatious eyes and great beauty. Instead of repudiating her, he raised a glass of red wine and toasted her. Others around the table joined him in the occasion.

Augusta then addressed the congregated guests, "Now that John has been put in his place, he can participate in the séance."

"William, you have been very quiet. Please explain your silence."

"Lady Gregory, ever since we entered the room, I've been hearing voices outside. I am sure it is only my imagination."

"William, don't tell me you are expecting spirits to arrive without being called by Mrs. O'Malley. If that is the case, her powers are indeed extraordinary."

Mrs. O'Malley responded in polite tones, "Lady Gregory, I make no claim to what I can or cannot do. The ability to speak to the dead and seek their advice or consolation is as much dependent upon those who are present as it is upon my ability to summon that which we cannot see in our own physical realm."

"Mrs. O'Malley, what you have said to me is that you have arrived at Coole Park with no guarantees. That is very honest of you."

"I think that all of you will be interested in what occurred at Baron and Lady Winslow's estate," said Olivia. "Prior to the séance, Mrs. O'Malley and I entered the library of the estate and immediately noticed that two young children of her ladyship's were playing a game. Both the brother and sister, however, were completely silent as they placed their hands on a numbered and illustrated board that had been placed upon the floor. Standing next to them was the youngest daughter of Lady Winslow. She appeared to be very frightened."

Olivia continued, "I asked the young girl why she was trembling. She told me her brother was going to ask the spirit board if there was a ghost in the library. I believe Americans call it a Ouija board. There were rumors of a ghost by the name of Jane McKnight who walked about the castle house. She was a servant who had killed the lord's children a hundred years previously in the castle. Jane was tried in the chapel and executed on the grounds of the estate. Before being executed, it was told she pleaded for her life in the very library where the children had congregated; the room having been converted from the former chapel.

"I noticed that both the brother and his sister had placed their hands upon the heart-shaped wooden planchette. When the young boy asked if she killed the lord's children, the planchette suddenly sped across the table to 'no.' The young man then asked it to spell the name of the spirit present. It is difficult to believe, but it spelled 'Jane McKnight' as quickly as my words are now reaching you."

"Olivia," said Augusta, "I am sorry to inform you and our guest that we do not own a spirit board nor do I intend to purchase one. It, like too many things spiritual, is subject to trickery. I suspect that the brother had great pleasure in frightening his little sister and in amusing both you and Mrs. O'Malley."

"Lady Gregory, what is the difference between this séance and a Ouija board? Don't they both depend on trickery?" No more had Olivia spoken these words than she realized the seriousness of her mistake. Augusta did not respond but only looked at William for a reaction.

"I shall answer that question, Olivia," said John Synge in a quiet voice. "We all wish there were something beyond ourselves. We have an innate fear of separation and an inborn need to be ruled. Lady Gregory has already forced me to admit that I can only be an agnostic based upon the simplicity of her argument that I cannot exist everywhere at once. I can, therefore, not support with absolute faith your proposition that the desires of the participants drive both the planchette and the séance."

William interrupted, "There, I heard the noise once more coming from the yard."

Olivia spoke, "William have I frightened you with my story of the three children in the library? I must assume to have at least made you edgy."

"Olivia, I must admit my imagination is more Irish than English. I think it comes from my acquaintances that still believe in fairies. After all, theirs is a rich heritage I am enamored with. Have you ever walked down a lane and felt the presence of another yet unknown and unseen by you?"

"William," said John, "you are just talking common sense. Of course, we all have looked over our shoulder when walking alone. It is part of Darwin's 'survival of the fittest' concept. That we have only survived by constant and careful vigilance. Have you not noticed how a cat's ears move though no sound is heard?"

"Your illustration is not convincing." Olivia smiled. "The cat hears what we cannot. Mrs. O'Malley, you have studied the role that the physic plays. Please tell us what you think."

"Please, I am no expert regarding what a cat can hear," responded Mrs. O'Malley. "I do believe that a cat senses a presence not known or seen by us."

"Perhaps we should ask a cat to join our séance." John laughed. "Lady Gregory, have you selected the subject of tonight's séance?"

"May I interrupt?" said Olivia. "If no subject comes to mind, I suggest we contact the servant of Bellgrove Park. After all, she was willing to move the Ouija board. She would make, I think, a most entertaining subject."

"I am sorry, Olivia, I do not know of whom you speak."

"Jane McKnight was executed at what is now the home of Baron and Lady Winslow. I am curious about whether or not she actually killed the children as charged by the magistrate. The fact that she was executed at Bellgrove Park was a most unusual accommodation for the grieving and vengeful family."

Augusta replied, "Is that agreeable with all of you?" Hers was a question to which no one responded.

"Mrs. O'Malley, is there anything else you require?"

"Yes, please ask your servants not to add wood to the fire. We do not wish to have any distractions. In addition, please have them snuff out every other candle that is now burning. I desire that no candles be left aflame on the east wall of the room. I also require one candle to burn in the center of the table. I will also need a large piece of paper to write on and a pen and an inkwell."

"As you wish," replied Lady Augusta.

As the staff carried out Mrs. O'Malley's wishes, the room became cooler and much darker. The ticking of the tall hall clock, that had not been noticed previously, seemed to sound much louder.

"Perhaps it is the coolness of the room, but can we do anything about the drafts of wind now moving the drapes?" asked John.

"John, only you would feel a draft." William laughed.

In the dimness of the large chamber, each guest took the hand of the ones adjoining them. William held both the hands of Olivia and Augusta, with their elbows resting on the table.

"When I call forth Jane McKnight, I will ask you to raise your elbows. Then close your eyes and concentrate with me," instructed Ms. O'Malley.

Moments past as all the guests pretended to concentrate. William could not help but smile when Olivia squeezed his hand while Augusta's hand remained constant and cool to the touch. The fire made a last crackle as the dying embers emitted smoke that curled as it rose within the firebox. The ticking of the clock vanished into silence.

"Jane McKnight, Jane McKnight, please join us in this séance?"

The arms of the participants began to feel heavy as they waited.

"Jane McKnight, Jane McKnight, I call upon you from the other side to join us." Suddenly Mrs. O'Malley moaned; at first just a slight whimper.

Each person seated at the table opened their eyes and stared at her.

Her face appeared ashen; her pupils had vanished as she rolled her eyes upward. The moaning increased in intensity and then she was silent; her head fell forward as though in exhaustion. She then reached for the pen and began to dip it repeatedly into the inkwell; spilling black ink not only on the paper but the tablecloth as well.

Each guest was spellbound by what was taking place. Mrs. O'Malley took the pen again and this time forcefully wrote on the page in mere fragments of words: "Blood, innocent, execution." Over and over she wrote the same three words.

Suddenly a loud sound came from the front door. It was as though a large rock had been thrown at the entry portal followed by a breaking sound. Everyone thought immediately that a stone had been thrown through a window in the entryway. Mrs. O'Malley immediately returned from the trance looking startled.

"What is going on?" Augusta shouted to the staff still waiting in the shadows of the large room.

"Madam, we don't know!" shouted Thedadus O'Flaherty, a kitchen servant. It was apparent that neither he nor the other members of the staff wanted to go near the door.

"I will go see what has happened!" William said.

"William, my beloved, please be careful!" Augusta said without thinking. For a moment, all the guests virtually froze at her words.

"I will." He rushed to the door. Immediately, he felt heat coming through the wooden door. "Fire! Fire!" he shouted.

Augusta screamed, "Water! Water! Get all the water you can carry!"

William opened the door as Thedadus threw two small buckets of water on the flames. Immediately, William ran to the stairs that led to the kitchen at the lowest level of the house. From there he drew water into a large copper pot and carried it back up to the door. Then he removed his outer woolen coat and dipped it into the water. Immediately he fought the flames, beating them into extinction. It was obviously a petroleum-based fire. With each strike of his coat, the flames lifted into the air as though glued to tar. Soon John was also assisting William and the others as they beat the fire into submission. All that remained was the lingering acid smell of the smoke.

Olivia looked towards Augusta. "What happened?"

"What I have long feared," she replied.

Olivia looked inquisitively at Augusta, her question still unanswered.

"It is a storm that is coming to Ireland like the black walls of rain that approach the Aran Islands. The storm that cannot be stopped by hangings at Kilmainham Gaol though rows of graves be filled with Ireland's youth. It is a war against English domination. Sadly, I understand though it was my own home they have chosen to burn."

"But Lady Gregory, you are English and dominate no one," Olivia spoke with conviction.

"It is a rule of nature; those that dominate will soon be dominated by the oppressed," Augusta replied. "Look at

Thedadus, though stronger than John, he worked half as fast as John did to save Coole Park. Why do you think he reacted so slowly? He is Irish and his heart is Irish as well. His father and his father before him worked this land yet they did not own it. These estate houses are symbols of what they consider to be the oppressor; regardless of the good or the evil committed by the owner."

Augusta continued, "We can see our future in what was known as the Confederate States of America. There is nothing that can be done. We await our own extinction."

William walked over to the two ladies; he appeared exhausted. "Augusta, I am concerned about your safety. People like William O'Brien are calling for the people to take action. There is no place safe in Ireland for those that truly love their country and have the wisdom to direct its course of future action. The call for revolution has been coming in various waves since the 12th century. While some may see it as a conflict of faiths; it is, in truth, a conflict over the ownership of land."

They returned to the drawing room to gather the possessions they had left behind in their rush to the door. Olivia stated emotionally, "Look, words have been added to what Mrs. O'Malley wrote while in a trance! I swear she had only written, 'Blood, innocent, execution.' Now added to the words are 'Lady Winslow.' What could that mean and who could have written it? Could the mother have killed her own child? Surely not, no indeed, such is not possible."

After Olivia's unanswerable question, Augusta slowly walked towards the library.

William joined her at the entryway and closed the door; locking it against all intruders. "Augusta, you have now made our relationship public by your words. I applaud you for your bravery. Not only did the guests hear you, but the staff did as well. Some may outwardly say that you spoke of platonic love, but all who were present know the truth. They can see it when I look into your eyes."

"William, I did not even realize what I was saying at the time. The heart alone spoke."

"I would that it was true that your boldness would take flight to all the steeples in Ireland. Our love should be made known through verse, song and play!"

"Please be patient, my love. You cannot wait any more than the Irish people can for what they believe in. Do you not know that both they and we shall be consumed by our passion? We must feel with our hearts but act solely based on our reason."

"Augusta, I would that it was so but passion cannot coexist with reason. You speak of a symbiotic relationship that does not exist." With those words, he embraced her placing her hips on the wide mahogany desk. His hands then moved to unlace her corset freeing her from all restraint.

❧21❧
Wales

Time passed quickly from the night intruders had attempted to burn down Coole Park. Affairs in Dublin kept William very busy. His literary reputation was beginning to be assured. Poems and plays continued to stream from his pen. It was as though he had obtained total command of poetic thought. Even as he walked, sentences would come to him as poetic expressions. His thoughts, however, drew him back to Coole Park and to the love that now consumed him.

He returned to Coole Park late in night when the sea clouds had given birth to a storm. Soon undressed, he found himself in the arms of Augusta.

The morning came too soon. They both turned in the large four-poster bed to watch the sun appear above the seven woods of Coole. The awakened ravens appeared only as black silhouettes against the changing stained-glass sky of the Irish morning. Small whiffs of fog rose from the many turloughs of the estate. Other woodland birds sang loudly to their guests.

"My beloved Augusta, since our love will eventually be known to all, let us journey to Holyhead where we might be alone."

"William, I have already explained to my staff that I was only speaking out of concern for your safety. Our other guests will have assumed the same. All of them will never believe that you, a man younger than I and so handsome, could truly care for me. I am but a plain woman; a fact that no amount of costly clothing or jewels can compensate for."

"If that is true, then why have I offered my love to you?"

Augusta spoke in soft words. "If we go to Wales, we must travel separately and meet only once we have arrived at our final destination. A friend of mine owns an estate in Wales. I will send her a telegram asking her to suggest a place where I can go alone and remain unknown. I will tell her I want to write and need to remain anonymous. Oh yes, it must offer us views of the ocean for we must awake and look upon the Irish Sea."

Lady Gregory always felt refreshed after her stay at the Shelbourne Hotel in Dublin. A magnificent hotel with its brightly painted bricks and front doors made of natural wood that opened into a cavernous, but exquisite, entryway that ended in a grand staircase with candles lit upon its post. It was her favorite hotel in that it overlooked what she considered to be Europe's grandest garden square, Saint Stephen's Green.

She enjoyed a fine meal of lamb at the Number 27 Bar & Lounge; one of the most beautiful restaurants in the city of Dublin. She sat with her back to other visitors so as to reduce the number of acquaintances she might encounter.

Augusta felt a light touch upon her shoulder. "Augusta? It is you. William said you would be traveling through Dublin on your way to England. How fortuitous that I should find you here at the Shelbourne."

"Ezra, how nice to see a familiar face," Augusta said with a warm, welcoming smile.

"I understand you had a problem at Coole Park. These are dangerous times for those living on estates in the countryside. There is a great deal of unrest developing here even in Dublin. The Irish are increasingly demanding that their ancestral lands be returned to them. They want to own the soil that they work. Without meaning to offend you, Lady Gregory, I understand their plight and sympathize with their cause," said Ezra in a serious tone.

Lady Gregory looked upon Ezra as a fellow writer whose talents were yet to be developed. Despite his youth, she realized the truth in his statements.

Ezra added, "I earlier saw Lady Rathburn in the lobby. I assume she will be joining you shortly?"

"While I am sympathetic to the landless poor, I do wish they would be more selective in whose house they burn. Regarding your earlier question – no, I intend to retire early this evening. The trip from Coole Park to Dublin was more tiring than I had expected it to be."

At her words, Ezra departed from her company. The warmth of the restaurant fire felt good to her. She tried not to think of the past but to only anticipate the future. She knew that if she lingered too long at desert, that someone else uninvited would wish to join her. While fame was yet to arrive, she was becoming increasingly well known among the social elite and literary figures of the city.

The train ride from Galway to Dublin had been a time to read and to write letters to her friends. She thought about her affair with William. "What a strange name, 'affair' to give to such intimate encounters?"

She had ridden by grand carriage from Kingsbridge Station to the Shelbourne. She went to bed early that night covered by fine, high-thread-count Egyptian sheets as she awaited the morning and her trip aboard the steamship *Sea Queen* to Holyhead.

Journey by steamer was far more comfortable and faster than by sailing ship. Third-class passengers still had to provide their own bedding and mess utensils, and their diet was still based on porridge and salt-cured meat. Fortunately for the poor, the trip to Holyhead was but a short journey. For those who could afford a high degree of comfort, meals were cooked and served by stewards. The cabins were lit by electric lights and heated by steam.

∂22∂
Passage

The steamer was loading freight when Augusta arrived at
the dock. The *Sea Queen* was a hybrid rig of both sail and
steam. Steam engines hissed as they lifted large crates high
into the air. Stevedores shouted to one another in the
potpourri of sounds that greeted her that Dublin morning.
The wind already felt cold. Seagulls screamed above as
though giving orders to the deckhands below. The workers
looked and performed as though they had just come from
the Temple Bar district after a night of whiskey and the
embrace of its women.

Lady Gregory wished to remain anonymous even
though her name was prominent on the list of passengers.
If asked, she intended to say she was going to take the train
in Holyhead on her way to visit relatives in England.

Once aboard the *Sea Queen*, she was led by a steward
to her freshly painted white stateroom. While traveling
first class, it appeared to be a rather small room. There was
a china water pitcher by the porcelain sink in one corner, a
writing desk, chair and a well-made bed. Since her cabin
faced onto the promenade deck, she enjoyed a large, wide
rectangular window allowing her to watch the guests as
they strolled; at night, shutters could be closed. Since the
wind was already gusting, she doubted if many would care
to sit in the canvas deck chairs placed alongside the wide
walkway.

"All ashore, going ashore," sounded loudly from the decks and was repeated throughout the ship. The *Sea Queen* soon sounded the backing bells, accompanied by three short blasts of the ship's whistle, as she eased herself stern first into the channel. A pusher boat pressed against the port bow aligning her in the easterly direction of Wales.

As she left the port of Dublin, Lady Gregory felt a strange feeling of both sadness and joy. There is something about a ship at sea that is both exciting and lonely; a feeling of togetherness and separation.

As soon as the *Sea Queen* left the outermost light on the spit, she began to roll in the swells of the Irish Sea.

Lady Gregory began to think once more about her life and the men that had entered into it both invited and uninvited. She thought of the prestige of her late husband, Sir Gregory, and how intelligent and kind he was. His inquisitive mind had attracted her just as strongly as the Adonis-like body of a younger man might a woman of less education. Then she thought once more of Wilfrid; the magnetism of his eyes and the lightness of his touch. How could she have risked so much for a man she truly did not know? Perhaps he represented an ideal she could love only in her imagination where reality does not tread. He had only remained a promise while Sir Gregory was a reality she could depend on.

Lady Gregory knew Wilfrid was not the kind of man to keep their affair a secret. She suspected that Sir Gregory knew of their passionate time in Egypt; after all, he had but to listen and only casually observe.

Now she was traveling across the Irish Sea to Wales to meet a man thirteen years younger than her. Their relationship while starting out as platonic had soon become one of passionate intimacy. As she looked out her window at the graybeards that struck the steamer, she wondered about what she doing. What attracted her to William so much? She knew the risk to her reputation and how the press would follow any type of scandal. Could they really remain anonymous in a foreign yet familiar country only a few sea miles from Ireland?

❧23❧
Holyhead

The sea began to flatten as the rolls of the ship decreased. It was nice not having to brace herself as she walked across the cabin to the water pitcher. Augusta poured some water on a small towel and slapped her face as though to awaken her reasoning to the events that had occurred and were about to happen.

Soon the *Sea Queen* was secured to her mooring bits with long lines of Manila hemp. Rat guards were bound upon the lines and a crowd had gathered to debark alongside the boarding latter that embraced the side of the steamer and whose base rolled loudly upon the wooden wharf.

A row of carriages awaited the guests as they or their servants solicited rides to the nearby railroad station to continue their journey to England. Few would spend more than one night in Wales, a country of stark natural beauty despite having become a victim of the industrial age with coal mining and black factory smoke.

Augusta knew, however, that once removed from the towns and mines, there were unpatrolled vistas of seascapes and mountains painted green by their forest and meadows; a land of abundant rain and cloud-pierced vistas.

Wales was a Celtic land with its own language, music and tradition. After leaving Holyhead, the carriage ascended into the low mountains where sheep grazed.

Further up the slopes were forests yet to yield to the woodman's axe.

The Blackstone Arms was the inn chosen by Augusta's friend as the perfect place to write in isolation. Its location far from any city and close proximity to the coast provided an ideal location for lovers who wished to rendezvous in secret.

The carriage stopped in front of a large Georgian inn that bore the sign "Blackstone Arms." Lady Gregory stepped from the carriage on the arms of a footman who promptly stepped forth from the inn; umbrella in hand for now the wind gusted from the sea bringing showers of rain with it. She stepped into the entryway to sign the registry. "My good sir, I see that William has already obtained us a room."

"Yes, Madam, your husband arrived earlier today."

Suddenly William was heard walking down the upstairs hall and entering the stairwell. Then on the staircase, she gazed up at him as he momentarily stopped to wave at her.

Augusta looked towards the innkeeper. "Sir, is the rain expected to last long into the evening?"

"Madam, Wales is the rainiest country in Europe. The closer you get to the coast; the more you can expect it to rain. However, I did see a Scotsman's coat a moment ago which means that the rain will soon end for the day."

"That makes me happy, for I wish to walk along the seashore towards evening. That is, if William will be kind enough to walk with me."

"Madam," said the innkeeper, "would you and your husband first care for some tea after I have taken your trunk upstairs?"

"Don't bother, Phillip," said William. "I will carry the lady's trunk myself," he said as he held Augusta's hand for just a moment before lifting her small trunk onto his shoulder.

Their room was at the end of the hall. As William opened the door, Augusta first noticed the view of the wild sea outside the three windows of the room. Then she looked at the deep red wallpaper of the chamber and the large mahogany four-poster bed with its enormous headboard. The room had a light, airy feel to it. Outside the window, the sea was spotlighted by a break in the clouds.

William, after placing the trunk on the wooden floor, looked into her eyes as he pulled her closer to him, his hands moving to free her of the restrictions of both her corset and chemise.

Outside, the rain continued to hit the panes carried by gusts of wind. The colonies of wild birds could be heard as a red kite swooped past their window. They held each other tightly awed by a force far greater than their own, or the world they had yet to know.

Like Ireland, Wales was a country where the twilight continued long into the evening. Even though they both desired to remain forever in the room, the thoughts of a walk along the shoreline with the tremendous breakers crashing upon the rocks lured them from their bed.

"Let us eat first and then walk," Augusta suggested.

The dining room faced a small formal garden filled with beautiful roses that were shielded from the wind by a low, moss-covered stone wall. Beyond the garden lay a cliff and then beyond that, the sea.

The innkeeper approached the table. "Madam, what would you and your husband care for?"

As Augusta held the large menu up, she smiled at William. "I would like the laverbread and a bowl of cawl cennin."

William added, "I would like the Welsh lamb, bara brith and a selection of vegetables from your own splendid garden. We would also like your Welsh cake for desert."

They enjoyed the steaming tea and scones that had earlier been placed upon the table, William spoke first, "You are the first woman I have been with that I could enjoy the silence of the day. I think that in the absence of speech, more can be spoken."

"Are you complimenting or condemning me as a poor conversationalist?" Augusta smiled.

"No, we communicate in so many ways. We feel the same warmth of the fire; hear the cry of the gulls that appear suspended on the updrafts of the cliff; and vividly remember the graceful flight of the red kite; yet we did not speak of these things. I think we communicate through silent thought; not outwardly spoken words. Have you ever noticed the house cat we mentioned before? She is continually bathed in sights and sounds not outwardly shared at the moment. Is that not how we write as well?"

"I accept your compliment though I wish to explore the matter with you later after our walk."

William spoke further, "The most intimate moments of our touch are not verbally shared, yet their meanings are fully understood by us both."

Augusta replied, "That is why I want us to walk along the beach. It is the sounds, taste and touch of the sea I want us to share though the breaking surf conceals our words."

The walk to the beach was an arduous one. The stone path was slippery with moss, many of the small stones dislodged by the heavy rains.

"Look!" said Augusta. "The sun has broken through the clouds and now once more spotlights the sea in its glow."

"It is a good sign indeed," said William.

Once upon the sand and rocky beach, they embraced and looked towards the horizon of the Irish Sea. Far out beyond the crashing surf, the distant shapes of sailing vessels could be seen. Further out, steamers with their myriad lights appeared as vessels continuing their journeys between the two islands of Great Britain.

They held hands while Augusta gathered periwinkles, mussels and cockleshells.

"Augusta, will their beauty endure beyond the beach?"

"How will I know if I do not gather them now? They will become memories to me, when you and I are parted, as we must soon be."

William replied, "You speak as though value should be placed in that not yet seen or heard. I will not leave you."

"Foolish man! Have you become immortal in our walk?"

"I will not depart from you though I die. For in your heart, I will remain till we are bound as one where spirits alone shall dwell. Did not the ring encompass us both?"

"How do you know we will still even be friends when we have returned to Ireland? Perhaps I will have grown tired of you by then." Augusta smiled.

"Yes, you are correct, we are all fickle and untrue even to the one that we love most. Regardless of what mistakes we make, we can never depart once we have loved. I do believe that lovers become one in flesh," said William.

There on the beach they remained as the small, lighted area of the sea vanished behind the swirling clouds of the approaching squall.

"William, we must hurry back to the inn," Augusta said as put the shells into her deep pockets.

The storm arrived with all its Welsh fury. The rain slammed against the windows and the stone façade of the inn. Small rivulets ran down from the panes. William arose from their bed to add more turf to the small fire.

They lay there secure in each other's arms. Tightly they held on as though they were defending themselves from the indifference of nature. Streaks of lightning hit the sea below them and sent its crashing echo throughout the room.

"I feel secure in the strength of your arms," Augusta said as she looked into his eyes. "That night you rushed to the burning door was a turning point for me. I knew that you were my defender, and that I would always be safe in your touch."

"You have given me a reason to live and, more than that, a renewed motivation to write," responded William. "My words from now on will reflect my love for you. This storm, from which we hide in each other's embrace, shall serve as a reminder of my devotion."

"William, you do not need to give reassurance to promises that cannot be kept. Soon we shall awake and return separately to Ireland. You will meet and love other women but please reserve a special place in your heart for me."

"What foolishness you speak. We are both unmarried. What rules of man have we violated? Should we not spend our lives together? If society demands, we shall marry."

"I cannot and you know that. My dream of a literary revival cannot be risked on an impulse no matter how noble it may be."

"What do you mean?" asked William, a tone of frustration in his voice.

"Ireland needs a literary revival if the traditions and voice of the Irish people are to survive."

"Do you mean that our not being together will be nobler than our love? Foolishness!" said William, growing increasingly frustrated.

"All my life," confessed Augusta, "I have wanted to make a difference and not to be just the wife of a famous person. I do not want to live or work in the shadow of another no matter how noble that person happens to be."

"Can we not share your love for writing and the Irish peasant?" asked William.

"I dream of a time when a theater will only perform the works of the Irish. England has its bard but who is Ireland's? Whose voice is given to those whose history is even richer with noble and enduring works?"

"A theater for the Irish? The peasants will have no interest for they are unlearned. Do you think the Anglo-Irish will care to attend? Please do not deceive yourself. Do not spend your life hoping for what cannot be," pleaded William.

"It can be if you will help me. I have the money, friends and position to make it work. You, Edward Martyn and I can write the works to be performed. Can your friend, John Synge not write as well? I have often heard you speak well of him. Perhaps even Ezra Pound could contribute in his own unique way."

"You mean write plays for an Irish theater?" asked William in a condescending fashion.

"Yes, write plays. You mentioned that you also know Maud Gonne. Is she not an actress of note?"

"Yes," replied William. "She is also a lover of the Irish people."

"If we dedicate ourselves to such a cause, we will have the plays and the stage talent to create a literary movement the like of which Ireland has never known."

"Where would this theater of yours be?" asked William.

"I don't yet know the exact location in Dublin, but there are many buildings we can rent or even purchase. I admit they may not all be in the best locations to attract crowds. A friend mentioned there might be a building on Abbey Street that could serve such a purpose."

"Augusta, I still do not know why we must remain as small children afraid of being scolded by their parents."

"William, I cannot be divided and bring this dream to fruition. We can work as partners. You can have lovers and still love me. I am willing to share you for such a noble undertaking."

"My beloved friend, no woman has ever said that and meant it," said William as he looked out the windows into the black void of the storm.

"William, I know you have needs I cannot fulfill. How can I expect you to remain faithful to me and your need to be with other women? It was very apparent that you were physically attracted to Olivia. How many more will there be? Let not my jealousy destroy what we have. Our working together will give legitimacy to our relationship as far as others are concerned. Late evenings spent with you and your friends will then be understood by all."

William rose from their bed and seated himself on a fireside chair; his eyes focused intently upon the fire. He wondered at how a woman who expressed such love, need and devotion could put so much at risk. Augusta sensed his thoughts. "Remember William, I am a widow. I am much older than you. Society will not accept us."

He did not speak as he reentered the warmth of the bed like a child reentering the womb of its mother. He lay upon his back watching the shadow play of flames on the wooden ceiling. Soon his eyes closed.

The morning came and with it the ending of the storm. A quiet breakfast and then she left the inn before him. He needed to wait for the next carriage so their departure would not appear simultaneous.

He felt his soul departing from his body. It was like a second death to him at that moment. Was he not worthy of her? Could she not understand that after they made love in the fairy ring, nothing could separate them from the need for one another? Into what hell had he been cast?

They did not meet on the trip to Ireland. Lady Gregory remained in her stateroom looking out her window at the sea while William walked about the decks. Later he went to the bar and ordered whiskey. There, holding, the small glass of brown liquid, he thought about Holyhead and Augusta. Had he been made the greatest offer in his life: a chance to write and have his works performed on stage or had he, as a man, been rejected by her, placed like a file inside a cabinet to be pulled when needed?

Upon the arrival of the steamer, he gathered his small trunk from the steward and walked down the catwalk to the pier. There he looked at the *Sea Queen* and for a moment, he thought he saw Augusta. A woman dressed like her looked in his direction but did not wave.

⁖24⁖
Dublin

As William walked along the streets of Dublin, he thought about his early life and his love for biology and zoology. He remembered his struggles with mathematics and languages as well as his difficulty with spelling as a result of having been born tone deaf.

"Yes," he thought, "I should have attended Trinity and become a doctor like several of my other friends; a life of calculated celibacy." Yet Augusta had awakened something in him that he could not control any more than his desire for her: a love of writing.

He thought about Maud Gonne. Had he truly loved her as well or was he merely infatuated by her beauty? She had already rejected him and the pain was renewed by Augusta's suggestion that she might perform in one of their plays. Even though he had desired Maud in the most intimate way, she had rejected his advances. Perhaps it was her refusal to submit that continued the pain within him. His pride had been hurt since their relationship and her refusal to marry him had become public.

Perhaps Augusta's offer of a clandestine relationship was more sensible; at least she wanted to protect their reputations. William's great sense of pride would be in jeopardy if he sought the favors of a woman too openly.

A drizzle was beginning to fall over Dublin. William entered Toner's on Baggot Street.

"Welcome William, good to see you," said the owner.

"Thank you, Alfred. It is good to be in Dublin."

"What can I get you? The usual, sir?"

"Yes, a sherry will do me fine." William was a man of habit. The only pub he frequented on his own in Dublin was Toner's. The only drink ordered there was sherry.

William was not outwardly social at Toner's. He preferred to sit with his back to the other customers, either reading a journal or writing on his notepad. Instead of the usual *craic* exchanged between the pub owner and a familiar client, there was only polite silence. After he finished his drink, he left to telegram Olivia. In his loneliness, he could not ignore the potential company of a woman.

Olivia responded quickly to his message: "I am at Brooks. Drop by." Brooks Hotel on Drury Street was one of the finest hotels in Dublin. It was conveniently located near St. Stephen's Green, Grafton Street, and Trinity College made it a popular location. As he entered the door, he placed his trunk in the care of the hotel valet and asked for Ms. Shakespear to be rung.

"Sir, who might I say is calling?" asked a staff member.

"Please tell her it is William."

"William who, sir?"

"William is both my first and last name."

"I understand, sir. I will send a messenger to her room."

"Thank you. Oh, by the way, please tell her that I will be waiting at the residents' lounge," William added.

He took the lift to the lower floor. There he entered the French oak paneled lounge with its, impressive library and large ornate mantled fireplace.

An hour later, Olivia entered through the door of the lounge. "William, this is indeed a surprise. I thought you might be composing verses with Augusta at Coole Park," she said in a teasing manner. "My friends tell me you two are a couple now."

"Olivia, I do not follow your line of reasoning."

"A very good friend of mine just happened to be returning from London on the *Sea Queen*. She said she saw both of you on the ship."

"Did she see us together?" asked William defensively.

"You must be in a relationship or you would not have asked such an irrelevant and very stupid question."

"Would it matter to you if we were?"

"Not in the least," Olivia responded.

"I thought not," replied William. Yet he could tell Olivia was not comfortable with the idea that he spent a weekend with Augusta.

"Where did my lovebirds stay while in England?" she asked.

"We were not in England," William replied.

"Oh, excuse me," said Olivia. "Am I to assume you ventured no further than Wales? Let me guess, no further than Holyhead. Your passion could not wait longer than a ferry ride?"

It was apparent to William that Olivia's pride had been deeply offended. It was obvious that she felt she had been used as a tool to make him even more appealing to Augusta than he already was. He now felt foolish about trying to be a contestant in a game in which no winner could emerge – a game of deceit, a fertile ground for vengeance.

"I am sorry, Olivia. I should have been more honest with you. I did not intentionally mislead you. What happened between us was genuine. You must admit we both shared the passion we felt that evening."

"I came into your arms believing you desired me as a woman not as an instrument of your lust for another. I feel compelled to speak to Augusta to save her from more of your ill-thought-out plans. Women are not tools to be used and then cast aside at your convenience once we have exhausted our function."

"Olivia, please forgive me," said William.

As he spoke, she looked intently at him. "I would have made a great lover and a friend."

"I know," he replied.

At that moment, he knew there was a strong possibility she would cast him as a character in one of her books.

❦ 25 ❦
Skellig Michael

With the intent of visiting a friend in Galway, William arrived at the train station and immediately went to the Kings Head where he met John Synge. He had been lodging with friends in County Sligo.

"John, good to see you again," said William as he entered the pub.

"William, I just started a play I would like to share with you once it has been completed."

"Fine, just send it to Dublin when you have finished the draft. I look forward to having a chance to read it. I know Augusta will be pleased as well."

"Edward mentioned to me about the firebomb at Coole Park. I think it scared him since his estate is not too far off. We talked about how Ireland is changing. I think the industrial revolution is playing a part here just as it has in England. The lower classes are becoming organized and very resentful of those of us who own property. As Lady Gregory found out, it does not matter how you are viewed on a personal level by the rebels, whether friend or foe. If you are rich and landed, you are their enemy by default."

"John, you are correct. The railroads, highways and telegraph have made us all one neurotic family. I long for the quiet of the countryside and a more simple time when a gentleman could sit by a trout stream and not be concerned for his life."

"I guess we are all dreamers," responded John. "The time, just removed from us, always seems the most desirable. We both agree that the future is uncertain and that time will bring an end to our style of living. I know it cannot be stopped. I think that is why I love to write. I, like you, feel that it allows me to capture the vanishing moments of our time."

John continued, "I can never thank you enough for encouraging me to visit the Aran Islands. I must admit that at first I was concerned about the isolation and loneliness such a barren island can produce within a man's soul. After I became used to it, I began to enjoy it immensely. It was one of the few times I was able to write uninterrupted. In fact, I think it was one of my most creative periods. As I have already mentioned to you, I enjoyed hearing the residents speaking to one another with their strong accents. It was as though I was an unseen presence. The young women would go about their work gossiping; flirting with the young men who worked nearby in the fields. I remember their loud talking when hanging laundry like there were no others present. I was simply a vision they had accepted like the sea and wind."

"John, I am thinking of stopping by Coole Park and checking on Augusta. Ever since that incident at the house, I have been concerned about her."

"William, don't get attached to Coole Park. It is too idyllic and you might not want to return to us."

"My carriage will soon be departing from Eyre Square," replied William.

"William, I wish you Godspeed. Please say hello to Augusta for me."

William left the pub and walked to Eyre Square, arriving just as the coach was loading its final passenger on its way to Gort. The passage to Gort was pleasant with clear skies and rising breeze. The branches of the overhanging limbs moved rhythmically in the wind. Only a few isolated clouds had gathered when the driver arrived at Coole Park.

A staff member approached William and extended his hand to take the small traveler's trunk. "Thank you. I know that Lady Gregory is not expecting me, but since I was in Galway, I thought I would pay her a visit."

"I am sorry, sir, but Lady Gregory is not currently in," he replied.

"Will she return soon?" William asked.

"I am not certain, sir. I expect her within two or three days. Do you intend to remain at Coole Park until she returns?"

William assumed she was visiting Edward or another nearby estate. "Perhaps I can join her if she is nearby."

"Sir, she has gone to County Kerry. You know how her Ladyship loves to collect stories. She was told a fascinating story about Skellig Michael. She became so interested in it that she wanted to see the island for herself."

"How long ago did she leave?" asked William.

"Probably not more than an hour or two ago."

"Oliver, will you arrange for your driver to take me to Gort? If I find her there, I might accompany her on her travels. I have myself always been interested in Skellig Michael."

"As you wish, sir."

William was disappointed when he arrived at Gort. He half expected to see Augusta there. Instead, he found out that she had departed only thirty minutes before his arrival. The next carriage going to County Kerry would be four hours later.

He sat on a wooden bench in the city park while waiting. At first, he felt ill at ease sitting in a public area.

He knew that any stranger in a rural community drew immediate attention followed by inquiries related to the purpose of the visit. Most villagers would assume that the purpose of such a visit was to see a relative. This in turn would lead to lengthy discussions related to the health and wellbeing of the relative.

William did not want to talk to anyone as he watched the leaves of the yew tree moving in the strong wind. He enjoyed looking at the beautiful red and yellow flowers, both wild and planted, and listening to the sound of flowing water in a nearby stream. Even the sound of flying insects, especially the sight of dragonflies, comforted him in their familiarity. The sun felt warm and relaxed him further as he sat.

He thought about the stone island far off the coast of Ireland that had drawn outcasts and seekers of God for centuries. As he recalled from his study of history, the island was occupied as early as the 8th century and then abandoned hundreds of years later. What stories could possibly have attracted her to such a desolate and unoccupied place?

There were, to be sure, monastic ruins on the island. Folklore told of an Irish King that fled to the island as a place of refuge. He vaguely remembered a saint who also founded a monastery on the island just five hundred years after the crucifixion of the Lord at Mount Calvary. William knew such islands would attract anyone interested in the history of Ireland and its spiritual nature.

Soon William found himself traveling the winding and bumpy roads of the Ring of Kerry. After a brief rest in Cahersiveen, he traveled to the village of Portmagee by donkey cart. Then to An Caladh, a village that separated the ocean from the hills and mountains of Kerry. Once in the village he entered a pub to inquire regarding a skiff to take him to Skellig Michael.

"Can any of you gentleman tell me how I might be able to hire a boat to take me to Skellig Michael?" William asked a group of twelve men who were sitting smoking their pipes around three tables. They were obviously involved in some type of card game. No one responded.

William repeated, "I would like to hire a boat to take me to Skellig Michael."

"You must not be from around here." One of the men spoke up, his face hidden under a flat cap.

"Sir, I am not from here. That is true. A woman may have made a similar inquiry a few hours ago. Do any of you remember a small woman most likely dressed in black?"

"I do. She, too wanted to go to Skellig Michael. I suggested she see Father Michael at the church. He is the only man I know that would be willing to take anyone out on a day like this. Indeed, he may have some spiritual connection with the dead monks that lived on the island centuries ago. Some say they can hear the Father talking to them after Mass. He is a strange fellow indeed."

"Is there something wrong with the weather? It is still warm enough and the sky does not look threatening."

"Stranger, above that ridge, the wind is starting to howl. Did you not see the mackerel sky the other morning? Have you not heard, 'Mare's tails and mackerel scales make tall ships carry low sails?' Some say it will be dry, not I. The sky this morning was a burning ember when the sun broke free of the mountain. It will not be too long before the clouds appear and the sea boils."

William could feel his own heart beating more rapidly. He recalled how he had learned to sail many years ago on a glacially formed lake in the Wicklow Mountains. He remembered his own small wooden boat capsizing when a strong wind blew through the valley; yet the day was clear and the sun most bright. Inwardly he feared that

Augusta was not aware of what was about to happen. "Will any of you rent me a small boat?" he asked.

"No, none of us are that foolish. We take care of our boats here. It is our livelihood. I will, however, sell you one. That way you will not have to return her," he said while the others laughed. He could hear some of the men saying he would turn around by the time he cleared Portmagee Channel, if he even made it that far.

William paid for the boat in English sterling. The man took him to where the small boat lay on the beach sand. It was an old boat of clinker construction with one plank overlapping the other. The boat was partially filled with water; a small crab strolled sideways across its sandy bottom. "This boat has not even been bailed out," William commented.

"If you want her to float, the water swells the wood that keeps the seams tight. Are you certain you know something about boats and sailing? The ocean out there is not like a lake or harbor you know. Good men die out there."

The wind was now whipping the canvas sail secured loosely to the mast and boom. "Help me bail her out, and then we can push her off," the former owner said loudly above the wind.

Soon William found himself straightening an assortment of lines and halyards as the small boat caught the wind in her teeth. A rooster tail of foam followed the boat through the channel, past the light and into the open Atlantic. Perched far out on her beam, William attempted to keep the boat on an even keel; spilling wind from both the mainsail and the jib as necessary. The rudder felt heavy in his hand as he struggled with the lines while being keenly sensitive to the heeling of the boat.

In his mad dash through the harbor, he had not paid attention to the cloud mass building just off to the west.

He could see the phantom-shaped island of Skellig Michael when his small craft crested a swell. There between him and the island appeared, for only a moment, a small boat heeling before the wind. He was not sure if it was indeed a boat or simply the spume being blown free from a graybeard. He continued in his pursuit of what he had seen; for what he thought and hoped to be both a boat and the island.

Soon, no matter how hard he tried, he could not see the craft upon which the priest and Augusta had ridden into the storm. The island appeared like the fingers of a giant emerging from the sea. The gray sandstone and sheer cliffs were covered in low hanging, swirling clouds. William could occasionally see myriad numbers of birds searching the sea for their food.

Again, his skiff crested an enormous wave of rogue appearance. He felt a sense of both despair and panic as he could not see the small boat in which, he assumed, Augusta was a passenger.

Then before him was the wreckage of a sailboat rising upon the swell. Clutching to a halyard was a small figure desperately holding onto the railing for her life. He could see no other survivor.

"Augusta, Augusta!" he shouted into the wind. She did not react to the approach of his small vessel for now the wind prevented any other sound to emerge.

As he passed only one or two meters from the capsized boat, she turned towards him and shouted, "William, my William!"

"Augusta, I will head the bow into your boat. Take the line I cast to you and tie the skiff to the wreckage." He quickly secured the line to a ballast weight that would, he hoped, allow him to cast it into the wind. He threw the line with all his strength as the boat crashed into the wreckage. It held fast allowing him to grab the arm of Lady Gregory.

With the strength that only dire necessity provides, he lifted her from the water as his bow crashed once more onto the wreckage. He held Augusta tight, releasing her for just a moment in order to cut his skiff free.

"Where is the Father you were with?" William shouted as his boat fell away from the other.

"Drowned, William, drowned!" she shouted.

"Are you sure, Augusta?" he shouted back at her.

"Yes, yes, I am sure."

"The sea is rising too fast, we have got to attempt to land on Skellig Michael and wait for the storm to exhaust itself."

"William, do what you must!" she said, collapsing beneath the gunwale of the boat.

He let the boat fall off enough to catch the wind. She heeled strongly to starboard as the sails caught the full force of the wind once more. He adjusted the halyards just in time to prevent her from turning turtle in the wild sea. The screaming wind prevented further communication until they entered the lee of the strangest and most beautiful of all the islands that he had ever seen. Puffins, skuas, great shearwaters, and sooty shearwaters flew about their heads as though they were being formally greeted by the island residents.

William and Augusta looked up in amazement at the sheer sides of the island; the verdant outcrops of grass, wild flowers and herbs that clung tenaciously to its vertical stony slopes.

"I don't know if the anchor will hold this bottom and soon it will be too dark to sail. We must try to anchor and then make a fast swim to shore making sure we stay clear of the pitching boat. Augusta! Can you swim?"

"I think I can remember how. My energy is gone. Please stay with me!"

"I will, I will!"

"Take off all your heavy garments for they will only weigh you down," William shouted.

A large swell lifted the boat and slammed it into the sandstone side of the cliff. Then as the skiff fell back into the grasp of the sea, its back now broken, both William and Augusta were thrown into the churning sea. Not wanting to see if she could swim and desperately fearing their separation, he grabbed and turned Augusta on her back. Grasping her in his forearm, he swam towards a narrow beach of pulsating smaller waves. Soon their feet were touching the kelp, rocks, and shells below.

Wet and cold, they looked at each other as rain fell upon the sea; a drenching, cold steady rain. They both knew they had to take shelter quickly. Above them were the 700 stone steps that the monks had laid or chiseled over a thousand years previously. Wet, moss-covered steps that appeared like the rungs of a sea ladder that had been hung against a vertical wall of stone.

Without speaking, they began their dangerous ascent. They did not know what to expect as they ascended. Suddenly the rock beneath Augusta's feet gave way and she slipped past William. Only his outstretched arm prevented her rapid descent to the edge of the cliff and certain death upon the stones at its base.

Dressed in rain and soil, she smiled at him. "Thank you. Thank you, my love."

After more than what seemed like an hour of arduous climbing, they arrived just below the summit at the abandoned monastic settlement.

"Augusta, look! Someone has been here recently and built a fire," William said as he looked at the partially burned wood.

"Could it have been the Father that was with me?" she asked.

"I think you are correct, for only a person of deep faith would come here."

Augusta said quietly, "Then I will pray for him."

They entered the larger of the stone beehive huts. There, in the swiftly arriving dusk, they looked about at the walls and ceiling of the structure. William spoke, awe in his voice. "I can't believe that no wood was used in the construction. The ceiling, walls and floor are nothing more than slabs of hewed stone. Not a drop of water has fallen from the ceiling yet the rain is descending upon us as though bedsheets of moisture were spread upon the roof."

A small stack of driftwood and peat stood in a corner. The greatest of the benefits were small sticks that had been dipped in phosphorus allowing them, when struck against the stone, to flash into a brilliant intense flame that could light both the wood and peat. Also within easy reach were a collection of handmade books with coarse leather bindings as well as paper and pens.

"Now you know why I wanted to come here," said Augusta. "The priest was a collector of stories and the author of others. He said that if I wanted them, I could have the collection of stories and ancient books he kept here. I told him I would accept them on behalf of the people of Ireland only if he showed me the island that inspired his faith."

Augusta continued, "Neither he nor I knew that a storm was approaching. The restlessness of the birds should have foretold our plight. The poor father had no knowledge of the sea. Not even the boat belonged to him. It was left to the parish church by one of the parishioners."

From the opening of the beehive hut, they could see the storm and the sea far below. Streaks of white foam covered the backs of the great, slate-covered swells as they rushed onto the shores of Valentia and then on to the Ring of Kerry.

"I saw some woolen blankets he must have stored here in the event of a prolonged stay. We must remove our wet clothing," said William.

By the light of the burning peat, William took the priest's pen and began to write on the coarse paper words that he would later use when remembering that evening:

The Faith of Skellig Michael

That which is sought within the awakened hours of desire.
A visitor rejected by the restless dreams of night.
A montage of uneven thoughts that dwell upon the serrated edge of Skellig Michael.
To again renew my faith upon the cliffs of the holy isle.
Let not my beliefs roam like seabirds about the cliffs of barren rock.
May I be cast to the sea if not my prayer is heard.

I must of the moment seize that which I have sought by quiet pools and reflective prayer.
Loosen me from the past where lack of faith was toasted with drink and laughter;
The chant of dreams that seek peace within now fills the leaden cup.

There is that within me that longs for a vision beyond my sight.
Am I a part of that which remains unseen to be revealed where earth and sea unite?
I must accept the night into which I shall enter; condemned both saint and sinner.

With faith I must trust your love like the seabird the air upon which it flies;
A dweller who seeks the solitude of Skellig Michael.

My lack of faith pleases not myself or others.

Is not faith a requirement of true love?
The wine which we seek to drink I cannot toast with alone.
The wind carries my words aloft where clouds do dwell;
To gods unseen.

Have I not bowed in prayer before you?
Humbled upon wet stone I knelt to add my tears.
Is love but a weariness to bear,
A penitent to desire?

For only love can free and bring me back to thee.
I have sought you among windblown leaves and within quiet places and found you not.
Perhaps this barren isle of wind, bird, and towering seas shall bring me peace at last and thee.

With shadows playing on the walls of stone, William laid his pen down and looked at Augusta.

"William, please let me read what you have written," she said.

"It is only what I feel. I know it does not have the required rhyme that you or any other would expect of me. I just wanted to capture the emotions that flood me now, nothing more. When the sun rises over Ireland, I will tear these words apart and throw them to the wind and sea."

"Will you discard me, too someday?" Augusta asked.

The sun rose sharp and clear after the storm. Their clothes were barely dry as they dressed. Below them could be heard shouts from the anchored rescue boat at the nearby lifesaving station.

"Lady Gregory! Lady Gregory!" shouted the young officer.

"Yes, we are okay," she shouted to those approaching the cave-like dwelling.

Both William and Lady Gregory emerged from the beehive hut and smiled at the officer.

"We are safe and warm," said William.

"Thanks be to God," the officer said. "All of Ireland has been worried about your ladyship. Sir, I don't believe I know you."

"William," he replied in a quiet voice.

"We found the body of the priest floating in the bay. We really had very little hope of finding you both alive. The storm was very fierce, but now clear, mild weather awaits us upon our return."

"We are sorry for the priest. He was a very kind man."

❧26❧
The Meadow

"Facing almost certain death, what did the Father say to you on your journey to Skellig Michael?" asked William a few days after the recovery of the priest's body from the frigid waters of the west coast of Ireland.

Augusta looked at him for a moment and then away towards the Victorian garden. "He mentioned, as we began to realize the seriousness of our situation, that he did not fear death, only life."

"What a strange remark coming from a man who could see the force of a heightening gale," replied William. "Perhaps he sensed that the purpose of his life had ended before your arrival."

"When I asked him to explain what he meant, the storm was upon us," continued Augusta. "His face did not bear the expression of fear. To me he appeared to be calm as he worked the tiller and the lines of the small craft. I think he was only trying to save me, not himself. Wherever he is now, may he be at peace in God's presence, free from the fear and loneliness we all share."

"I am sorry to have brought up a subject that only brings sadness to us both. Augusta, let us go for a walk among the trees and meadows of your estate," said William as he finished his tea with Lady Gregory. "No matter how beautiful the house, I feel that there is always more life and beauty outdoors."

"William, are you becoming a poet of nature; a follower of Wadsworth?" she said with a smile. "Then you will keep company with Tennyson and Taylor and end up as famous as John Ruskin."

Augusta laughingly continued, "My friends have given John Ruskin an additional last name. They refer to him as John Ruskin Who." Even William laughed aloud with her.

"I shall be very careful of you." William smiled.

"I will be happy with you as long as you do not become like that depressingly familiar Henry David Thoreau of America. Even he had to return to society occasionally to escape being suffocated by the isolation of Walden Pond. While I have great admiration for the peasant class, I certainly do not wish to be landless."

"Augusta, you defend the lower classes like a viewer of art who stands before the painting not spattered by its paint and persistently aloof."

"I believe one can speak and write about reality without being a part of it." She laughed realizing that her argument had lost its credibility.

"Then it is time. Let's enter your woods, meadows and lakes like characters in Alice in Wonderland," he said as he rose from his chair and walked over to the hat rack.

"So be it, if you command. Shall I be Alice and you the Hatter?"

"Choose your words like one who selects a weapon before a duel," he returned.

She covered her tightly woven hair with a light yellow bonnet and selected a deep green parasol from the tall intricately carved wooden wardrobe. A wardrobe dressed with ivory inlays.

Into the brilliant sunlight they stepped. The odors of the garden surrounded them while butterflies perched upon Augusta's bonnet. As soon as they had exited the garden, they looked back towards the house and then immediately reached for each other's hand. Under their feet, smooth meadow grass bent softly. Distant fields looked lavender in their dress of purple-hewn grasses.

One butterfly remained resting upon Augusta's hat. "The butterfly atop your bonnet is as much in love with you as I," said William.

"Why is that?" she responded.

"It cannot let go of you anymore than I can. It has a need to be carried by you just as my spirit does."

"Do not flatter me too much, or I will not believe anything you say to me in the future." She laughed.

Soon they found themselves walking past one of the many turloughs that reside within the estate. Swans floated or swam upon the still waters creating double images of themselves. Soon wild ducks took flight as Augusta and William walked increasingly closer to the edge of the large turlough.

"William, what is going to become of us?"

"Augusta, you hold all of the cards. Only you can control my future beyond this day."

"I do not want you to appear weak. I love your strength," she replied.

"How can both strength and weakness be so intertwined? If you are threatened, my courage will prevail, but in your presence, beside these still waters, I am weak. Obviously my constant pursuit of you has availed me nothing," said William.

"Your words make me the fox before the hounds." She laughed.

"Unlike that which is wild, my pursuit is one of love. Tell me how to not love you, and I will obey you."

"William you are too sensitive both in your work and in your words to me. I do not want you to depart, nor do I want to obey you like a wife does her husband."

"I fail to see what is wrong with the love expressed between a married man and woman," said William defensively.

"Do you not know that marriage is but a license to be sanctified by the church and enforced by the law?"

"Augusta, it appears that our words are following two different paths," said William in a solemn tone.

"I would that there be no division between us. The difference in our sexes prevents our thoughts and emotions from being the same." She paused. "It is our diversity that draws us together. If we become as one, we will stagnate. Have you not noticed the turloughs of Coole? The waters in the month of August vanish from them only to return when the fall and winter rains come again to Ireland. The waters of these lakes are forever renewing; forever changing, and therein is their magic found."

"You divert my attention from the subject of most relevance to me. However, yes, I have often wondered why the water suddenly vanishes. That is a mystery that not even Edward can solve," William said with a reluctant smile.

"We are like that: free, renewing and ever changing," said Augusta.

Soon they found themselves deep in the woods of Kyle-na-no. The green boughs of the trees spoke as squirrels ran busily along the limbs; up and down the trunks of the large trees. Fallen leaves added their own sounds as William and Augusta walked on the wooded paths where limbs clasped one another overhead.

William looked at Augusta. "I feel that we are safe within this forest. Only nature surrounds and speaks to us. The eyes that look upon us are those of innocence. The squirrels that run so free, I feel, are protected from age, and these forests will remain as they have always been. Only we are the interrupters."

"Your words bring a meaning to these woods that I have not heard expressed before except within my own heart. I would that it were so."

Their walk among the trees took them to a sunny glade that adjoined a small turlough. Alongside the lake grew a large yew tree of great age. "If fairies exist and I believe that they do, they are here among us now," said William.

"There is so much that exists that we cannot see. If there be eyes that look upon us now, they are kind ones indeed."

They sat down on the lavender-tinged grass that grew abundantly upon the banks of the turlough. Augusta removed her bonnet and let the sun rest upon her forehead as she looked at the light streaming through the trees.

"Every day that I am alive, I am thankful," she said.

"What are you thankful for?" he asked.

"I am thankful for these woods and lakes. They give me comfort and meaning to my life."

"Is that all?" He smiled.

"No, I am thankful for this moment with you beside the still water. You are near my side, and I feel safe in your presence."

William looked at her great beauty, the intense rays of the sun upon her face and lips. The highlights in her hair radiated colors like those of an Irish field where wildflowers of varying hues abound.

"Is the water warm?" asked Augusta.

William bent over to touch the surface of the lake. His fingers created ripples that looked like broken stained glass within a church. He let his hand remain submerged for a moment for the water was very warm in the stillness of the day.

"Yes," he replied to her question as he shook the moisture from his hand.

"Then we should bathe in the lake," she said joyfully.

There upon the smooth grass they laid. As he cradled her head under his arm, they were profoundly at rest encased in sunlight and the perfume of wild flowers. The hours past too quickly and the warmth of the sun was soon extinguished by the shade cast by the trees.

"Let us dress and return to Coole House. There we can warm ourselves by the fire and talk into the late evening. I will have Oliver prepare a guestroom for you. You must stay the night with me."

"How can I refuse an offer to be in your presence?"

They began to dress surrounded by the sounds that accompanied the early mist of twilight's arrival. A large owl could be heard deep in the woods followed by a most unusual silence.

"Augusta, I feel a presence that is not of this wood."

"William, what do you mean?" she asked, an inquisitive smile on her face.

"I sense that someone is looking at us. I think the silence of the forest heralds that an intruder is present," he replied.

"William, you would have me believe that you possess a most unusual gift of perception."

"Perhaps, but I find that I need to obey whatever intuition I possess," he said quietly.

On the other side of the turlough, a branch snapped under the weight of a large animal. "Listen!" he said.

After a moment, she responded, "Yes, I heard that sound also."

Suddenly in the prolonged twilight of an Irish evening, forms began to emerge from the woods on the opposite side of the turlough. They appeared as blackened shapes until dressed in the dim light of a witch's moon.

"Who is there?" shouted William.

The shapes stood still holding what appeared to be rakes, hoes and sickles in their hands. The intruders seemed to be a small group of men. From the shadow of the yew behind them, a woman dressed in a full skirt appeared. Her features remained unseen.

Augusta whispered to William, "In a moment, let us prepare to run."

"Leave everything behind for we must run as quickly as possible," William instructed. "There are at least five men and a woman. I can't understand why they have not stepped forward. It is apparent they are awaiting the woman's command to pursue."

"Who could she be?" asked Augusta.

Just as quickly as they had emerged from the woods, they were gone having stepped back into the dark shadows of the forest.

William whispered, "Let us run now."

Immediately they both rose and began to flee in the direction of Coole House. Even though they did not look back, they could feel the presence of their pursuers. They sensed that they were gaining on them. Suddenly they entered the clearing in front of the estate.

"William, I must rest. I cannot run anymore," pleaded Augusta.

William stopped and turned her towards him; his embrace was one of strength. She knew she was safe within his arms regardless of what was to follow. Then William addressed the pursuers, "What do you want?" he shouted.

"Our land! Our land!" came the reply in unison.

William looked at Augusta expecting the blows of farm tools to follow. Instead there was only silence. He looked again, only the figure of a lone woman remained; her identity hidden by the darkness. Then she, too vanished from his sight.

"We are safe," said Augusta. "They will not pursue us now that we are this close to the house. One shout from me and my staff will come with guns. If they were going to kill us, they would have done so by the turlough."

"There are many animals in the woods this night," said William sarcastically as they walked towards the house through the moonlit garden. "Did you recognize the voice of the men or their silhouettes?

"No, I did not," responded Augusta.

"There was something vaguely familiar about the form of the woman," responded William. "I think our lives hung in the balance of her decision. I don't exactly know why, but I feel I must know her.

✦27✦
ℐalling ℛain

William was about to enter Dublin's Saint Steven's Green when he heard a loud sound from the street. A milk wagon had a wheel fall from the cart, spilling gallons of fresh, warm milk upon the cobblestones. As he observed the frustration of the driver, William looked towards the Shelbourne Hotel. There just emerging from the hotel was Lady Gregory. She was saying goodbye to a smartly dressed gentleman friend he did not recognize.

William quickly walked towards her, smiling. "Lady Gregory, I'm going for a stroll in Saint Steven's Green. Would you be kind enough to join me?" he asked.

"How are you William?" she said as they crossed the street to enter the park.

"Missing you, but you knew that already."

"We must be careful as we walk. Dublin is already alive with gossipmongers."

"Augusta, I still do not understand why you are so concerned. We are only walking. Those who must be gazing at us remain unseen, and I am sure, very disappointed in our lack of impropriety."

William continued, "I still do not understand your protracted period of morning. At times, I feel that you are competing with Queen Victoria in your wearing of black."

"Men do not understand the ritual of mourning. It is a complex interplay of emotions and propriety. I continue to worry that we would not only damage our reputations but the Irish theater as well. You understand that we still need investors in our joint effort. People will not invest if we get involved in a scandal. Reputation is the cornerstone of trust."

"Must the heart always be so hidden? There is no damage to be done with a quiet walk in this most beautiful of parks. Look at the swans upon the lake. They are no more interested in us than we are in them. Will our ignoring them make them less of a swan?"

"William, your words lack their usual organization. You of all men express yourself most eloquently, yet at this moment you falter."

"You judge me too critically. The passion we shared at the tower castle must now be shown only in words? I wish merely to tell you that I love you."

They strolled past the pavilion; past the couples reclining upon the grass; past the farmer's son playing the penny whistle and then stood on the stone bridge. The calm waters of the small lake tossed their images back at them.

"Are the reflections truly us, William?"

"Just as the wind alters our images upon this small body of water, there is little clarity in our lives. We, like the water before us, are changed by what alters the surface of our identity. Can the soul cast a reflection?"

"Perhaps, someday, perhaps," She laughed.

William picked a sunflower from the garden and handed it to Augusta.

"Had you picked a more beautiful flower, I would have refused it," she said.

"How strange your response to a gift from the heart," William replied.

"You picked a flower that none will notice except for me. Had you picked a rose, then you would have been offering your love in a most public and inappropriate fashion," she said.

"In France, Van Gogh paints sunflowers that are strikingly beautiful. Do not thank the humblest of flowers less beautiful than the rose. As you know, only the sunflower follows the sun. I feel that it is an act of worship and not a necessity born of indifferent nature," said William as he lightly touched her hand.

"My poet friend, you wish to give meaning to that which has none," she responded.

"You are wrong, Augusta. There is no work of nature or of god that is devoid of meaning if such be given to it by either a lover or a poet. Are not the two the same?"

"Then I shall accept the humblest of flowers and believe it to be the most beautiful of offerings, as though an Olympian god had placed it within my hand," she said with a coquettish smile.

They stood on the bridge and looked into each other eyes searching for that which cannot be expressed in words. William placed his hand once more upon hers while her hand rested on the cold, damp stone of the bridge.

"I find warmth in your touch," she said. "I would that you would cover my body now as the mother hen does her chicks. The wind that blows across the water is very cool."

William pressed his shoulder discretely against hers. "I would that we could stay here unseen except for the inquisitive swans. Augusta, you have made me aware of others even when they are not present. I sense that someone is staring yet I cannot see them," commented William.

"I also feel a presence. Our mutual feelings lend credibility to such a shared sensation." They looked around but could not see anyone except for the ill-defined form of a lady across the small lake. Mist was rising from the surface creating a phantom of her shape and masking her appearance.

"I sense that she is staring at us," said Augusta.

"I would rather think she is feeding the swans although none come to her," said William.

The mist had risen upon the lake early that morning. Images that would have been distinct were now diffused in the dim light of a Dublin morning.

"Usually the fog rises earlier than this. I am certain that the predicted rain will drive the fog from the park for the wind will soon shift to the southwest and increase. I have noticed that for a few days the weather has been somewhat unsettled," said William as he continued to gaze at the strange woman across the lake. "I heard earlier that a hurricane from the Atlantic will bring storms to Dublin."

"When," asked Augusta, "do you expect the hurricane to venture this far north? It was the topic of discussion during my breakfast this morning. Perhaps our cold waters will protect us from a tempest born in the warm, tropical seas.

"The only source of knowledge we have was that reported from a steamer that was able to make twelve knots per hour and could, therefore, stay ahead of the slow moving storm. I understand that the slower a hurricane moves the more violent it becomes."

A gentle rain began to fall. People throughout the park scurried for shelter. The wind increased as they spoke as the shower descended upon them. He once more looked at the strange woman. "You know what interests me most about our intruder is that I am familiar with the area of the lake where she is located. There are no paths that lead to where she is standing; only thick trees and tangled vines."

Augusta responded, "I wonder what she must be thinking about? It certainly is not about us. She probably just enjoys seeing rain fall upon the lake. I am curious though about her not raising a parasol. She does seem to have one in her right hand almost leaning on it as one might a cane."

William looked at Augusta as they shared her parasol. "Did you see how the flowers of the park are beginning to wear the tints of autumn? It is my favorite time of the year; reality is all but hidden.

William looked up at the sky, and for a brief time, he saw a small clearing in the clouds; for a moment, the shower stopped. Then he looked back across the lake. "Look Augusta, the sunlight has driven our stranger away. I will refer to her as the Woman of the Mist. Perhaps she was but a phantom of the park."

Augusta replied, "If she is but a spirit, I would think that she was seeking someone lost in the lake; a child perhaps or even a lover."

"Such sad thoughts, Augusta," replied William.

"I know, but don't we all seek the past; even when it is most painful to us?" she replied.

William responded, "You are correct, so much dwells there unseen by us yet waiting to be resurrected by a thought; a song or a child's playful cry. Is it possible that our Woman of the Mist never existed at all? She was perhaps just shadows among leaves; mist rising from water."

Yet within William's thoughts, an image of Olivia appeared. Even though they had been lovers for only a moment, she was ever present like that of a spirit now dwelling within his body. "No, it could not have been her," he thought. "Augusta was correct; the Lady of the Mist must have been formed only of shadows created by our desire to believe."

"Augusta, may I walk you back to the Shelbourne Hotel?"

"Yes, that would be nice."

As they approached the hotel, another party of guests was just stepping from their carriage. "William, I know that family well. Lady Ellen's husband was a friend of Sir Gregory."

"Do not be so concerned. You are a woman who guides the careers of many aspiring poets, authors and playwrights. It will not seem unusual for you to accompany such a writer to the hotel for dinner."

"I will have dinner with you against my better judgment," Augusta said with a smile.

As they entered the elegant dining room, Lady Ellen had just been seated with her younger daughter. When she saw Augusta and William, she beckoned them to her table. "Lady Gregory, how wonderful it is to see you. My husband and I have been so worried about you. Out there in the country with all the unrest that is sweeping Ireland. Surely the crown can send more troops to protect her majesty's people. I don't want the Irish peasants to be treated unkindly, but the crown's interest must be seen to first regardless of the cost in human suffering. The peasants depend upon our lands for support and our laws to protect them from harm. Don't you agree, Augusta?"

"Lady Ellen, you have spoken as the landed Anglo-Irish should. It is true they need our help but not our rule."

Lady Ellen's family had ruled over fertile Irish lands for centuries. Her English roots were well known as she frequently attended fashionable parties in London; such celebrity events were printed even in the penny journals of Dublin.

Augusta glanced towards William as they walked away from Lady Ellen's table. "William, I hope you don't mind, I have lost my appetite for a large meal. I would prefer just tea and scones instead. It saddens me that I must move within the circles of such people as Lady Ellen. Even though we have known each other for years, I feel compelled to address her as 'Lady' even in my own home."

"Augusta, I would not be so concerned about what she thinks. I predict that the class she represents will soon disappear from our island; and with it, the life you and I have known. Wealth is but a fickle visitor."

"William, that is true. That is why there is so little time for us to write and produce plays that will be meaningful to our beloved Ireland. You see, without our guidance and perseverance, the literature of Ireland will not be preserved. It will vanish in the fires of our great houses."

"Augusta, you are always in such a hurry. Can you not stop for a moment and be content? I fear for both your safety and your health. Has it not occur to you that the Woman of the Mist may be an informant tracking your every move, waiting for you to be alone and vulnerable whether it be night or day? The irony is we cannot be certain whether she is Irish or British for such are the times."

"How can I be contended while Ireland is aflame with revolution, and tyranny continues within our sight? I must continue to collect the stories of the people and publish them before they are lost. As you know, literature is how a nation defines itself; makes its identity clear to future generations."

William was beginning to be disappointed in the prospects of the evening. He had hoped after seeing Lady Gregory emerging from the hotel that they might enjoy a sherry and then be together as they had been before. While Augusta and even Maud Gonne were passionate about the events hurling Ireland into an uncertain future, William was not. He sought quiet moments of reflection and creativity. He sought that which was beautiful, like the woods of Coole Park, and not the fervor of an orator's call for conflict.

"Augusta, I must go and join John Synge for a discussion related to my review of his play. I hope you will forgive me."

"William, I will step to the entryway with you, so I can see the approaching storm."

There in the entryway of the hotel under a gas lamp, William pressed her body to his own. He could not help but kiss her lips in the glow of the gaslight.

As he looked up, he saw a woman looking at him from behind a curtain in the reception area of the hotel. It was just a brief glance as the curtain then immediately covered her face.

"Augusta, please be careful. I love you."

"William, I know."

William left Augusta under the lamp waiting only long enough to ensure that she had reentered the hotel's lobby. Then he began to walk in the increasingly heavy rain. After crossing Saint Stephen's Road, he reentered the park. He had decided to walk to Trinity to meet with John Synge as he had previously mentioned to Augusta. He had planned to meet him in a small anteroom just off the main library. There they could work in obscurity while being able to talk aloud without disturbing the other library clientele.

As he walked, William felt somewhat guilty in that he would have stayed with Augusta had she desired him to. His devotion to her exceeded all other obligations.

No sooner had he entered the park, he sensed he was once more being followed. He walked across the stone bridge and wheeled around to see who was pursuing him. The heavy rain now obliterated any sounds of footsteps. He could not see anyone in the dim glow of the gaslights. Then he saw a figure that seemed to be floating towards him; moving slowly but without the up and down motion of a person's pace. Suddenly he felt panic and began to run.

He found it impossible to hold the umbrella and quickly cast it aside as lightning lit up the sky reaching for the earth like the claws of a cat. Soon the rain felt like small stones striking his exposed face. He removed his glasses since they were rain-streaked and, therefore, provided no additional clarity of sight.

Soon out of breadth, he exited the park while maintaining a quickened step. He quickly found himself at Trinity College and immediately walked up the stairs to the library; a beautiful, immense paneled room holding the works of centuries of Irish and English writers. He soon found the anteroom, knocked upon the door and entered. The room was empty except for a plain table and two hard, wooden chairs.

"Perhaps," William thought, "the storm has discouraged John from venturing out into the evening. After all, his health is deteriorating and he, by his own admission, is increasingly subject to bouts of pneumonia.

28

The Fortune-Teller

In the dark alleyways of Dublin were those who tell fortunes. Dimly lit shops located away from the successful people of the city; for those who walked proudly along Grafton Street had no need to know their fortune. The gypsies read the cards and spoke while incense burned and light flickered within their shops as silhouettes danced to the flame of the candle.

Williams's disappointment in not finding John had sent him into despair. Not only had his plans with Augusta been shattered but also his hoped for discussions with Synge. He felt that good fortune was now alluding him if even but for a moment. People had realized his creative genius early, but failed to convince him of his unique gift.

"Perhaps there is something within me that can be changed?" he thought.

Outside the narrow shop was a small display window that held a stack of tarot cards placed upon a Quija board. He pulled the bell and then turned the handle of the front door to the establishment. There was a staircase that ascended to a second floor while to his right was a drawing room dimly lit by a kerosene flame.

"Hello, hello," he spoke softly for the room demanded silence.

Even though wet with rain, he sat down upon a soft chair with an almost vertical back. He looked into the flickering kerosene flame and thought about Augusta and the vision of the unidentified woman in the park. He wondered if an apparition had sought him in order to warn him of an impending event of great magnitude. Perhaps, he reasoned, a gypsy might be able to tell him who the person in the park was and what bearing upon his life she was to play.

William soon lost track of time as though hypnotized by the flame. Within his mind, he could see Olivia reaching out to him, cold and frightened as one who had drowned.

Suddenly the door from a back chamber opened and a young woman appeared. Unlike a person whose appearance had been stereotyped, the woman was smartly dress. While the dimness did not reveal her features with absolute clarity, it was apparent she was of Celtic origin.

"You came to me or to seek shelter from the rain?" she asked.

"I came to see the truth, yet I do admit I welcome the shelter as well. I apologize for being so wet. I know water must have dripped to the floor from my hat and coat. I am so sorry," he said.

"Please wait just a moment. The air is too cool and I need a shawl," the woman said quietly.

As he waited, William stood and read a poem hanging in a dark wooden frame on the wall.

The Reading of a Palm

Within the dark recesses of the alleys they dwell,
Readers of the palm and card.
Candlelight and incense
Fill their shops with eerie sights and scents.

Fortunes told by strangers in the alleyways of Dublin.

Beware my friend, do not enter.
Their eyes bewitch the vain and curious.

For a pound sterling, they will speak your hidden dreams.
No bad news to share, or threat of tears.
The business savvy know.

We all long to prosper and mature with years.
Yet your fortune is already read.
Not upon the palm
Or within the tea leaves spread upon a table.
It is written in the furrows of your thoughts.

Like the gypsy of the street.
We speak not the truth to one another.
Our destiny too easily read by a fortune-teller's stare.

I should have sought the tarot cards when first we met.
The future was too soon made clear.
The cost for my sanity but a coin
And the reading of my palm in Dublin.

"What a strange poem," William thought. "In truth perhaps it is my own sanity I am seeking."

"Sir, what shall I call you?" she asked.

"William is fine," he responded.

"Please sit down while I pour tea for us."

"That is very nice of you. Tea will take the chill from this cold, rainy night. I expected a hurricane to bring warmer showers," he said while looking down upon the dark floor to see his wet footprints.

The sounds of the clock and the pouring of tea were amplified in the dark, quiet room.

William continued, "To be honest, I was surprised that you were even open this evening. I feel certain that many will not want to venture forth in the rain."

"You are correct. This, however, is my home. I never know when a gentleman will seek my services in the night. We look inward into our selves when dusk first arrives. We are most alone when the night returns and the streets are silent. The lonely and the sad often seek a stranger."

As she sat closer to the flame, William noticed her long blond hair gathered into a tightly woven bun. Her eyes appeared to be a deep blue, but he was not certain of their color. Perhaps his imagination was providing details that were not present.

"You have come seeking your fortune?" she asked.

"Yes, but may I be truthful? It is not only my fortune I seek, but a moment free of solitude. The rain has increased my sense of isolation," William added.

"You can sit here until another customer rings," she said with a smile.

"Are you expecting another?" he asked.

"A messenger boy arrived just before you rang. He handed me a note from a woman, unsigned, asking if she could see me later in the evening. Strange, she did not mention any specific time nor did she provide me with information to inform her of my availability."

"Did you ask the messenger for any details regarding the woman?" William asked.

"He just said that he was hailed on Saint Stephen's Road and asked to deliver the message. I suppose she will be here sometime before midnight but that is only a supposition."

William could not help but feel ill at ease regarding the woman. "Surely, it could not be 'The Woman of the Mist,'" he thought.

The small turf fire provided shadows upon the furniture, walls and faces within the chamber. It was apparent that the teller of fortunes had but little money to heat the room. William felt his wool coat and noticed that little of the moisture had left it.

"I charge one pound sterling for reading the cards. If you prefer the Ouija board, it will be one and one-half pounds sterling."

"I recently toyed with the Ouija board, and found it somewhat amusing. I, therefore, prefer the use of the board," William replied.

"As you will, sir," she replied.

"First, I must ask you your name," stated William.

"Sir, my name is Mary."

"A strange name for a fortune-teller. I would have expected something far more exotic. Are you Irish?" William asked.

"No, sir, I am Polish."

"Yet your name is 'Mary.' I assume that you were born a Christian?" asked William

"Yes, sir. I am a Catholic."

"A strange profession for a Catholic," William said with a smile.

"Does not faith verify the existence of the soul?" Mary asked.

"Yes, it does," he replied.

Mary then continued, "When you came to my shop, you were troubled. I sense that it is not your health nor finances that concern you."

"That is correct. I keep having the sensation that I am being followed by a woman I cannot identify. Perhaps you can assist me in my quest to know who she is or even if she exists."

"I feel that a woman is calling you from a strange land. I will ask the board her name," said Mary as both of them placed their hands upon the heart-shaped planchette. "Woman formed only of mist, what is your name and from whence do you come?"

Slowly the planchette moved across the wooden board. Letter by letter it spelled the name "C-E-L-I-N-E."

"Céline, from which country do you come?" she asked.

Again, the planchette slowly spelled the letters "F-R-A-N-C-E."

Astonished, William sighed loudly as though a dagger had penetrated his stomach. There is no possible way she could know the name of the French prostitute he had loved in Montmartre.

"We must rest," said Mary who now appeared to be exhausted as she left the room.

William sat in the chair. A cool wind seemed to move through the room stirring the turf fire into a red glow. "Céline," he thought. "How could she know?"

⌒29⌒
The French Prostitute

Paris! It was everything the young William had hoped it would be as he stepped from the train that had just arrived at the Gare du Nord. Its beautiful boulevards and fine cabarets attracted young artists, poets and writers from around the world. He had come there to win the hand of Maud Gonne. Since his arrival, she had shown little interest in the fledgling poet. Despondent, he decided to stay a few more days since he had paid the rent on a loft apartment in the Montmartre section of the city. William had been enamored by the impressionist and post-impressionist paintings. Images that allowed the viewer to construct his own reality within the swirling paint, intense colors and blurred meanings depicted on the canvases. Art was what you saw and then experienced at the emotional level; yielding an almost infinite variety of interpretations as varied as the viewers themselves.

Of the impressionists, William admired the work of Edouard Manet the most. The painting, 'Olympia,' held his attention in bondage. The eye contact of the courtesan in the painting captivated him and would not let him go. William felt that he could hear her eyes; a language spoken by physical expression. The model's eyes spoke to his deepest longings. He desperately wanted to find the model, Victorine Meurent, though he knew she was now much older than he. William realized that his dream was truly not the woman as a physical being but as an image of his inner desire.

After leaving the Musée d'Orsay, he walked the windy streets that bordered the Seine. Then he caught a trolley to Montmartre where he had rented an apartment. He looked up at the empty windows above the street and decided to walk further up the hill to any cabaret that was open where music cascaded to the streets and voices could be heard. He heard an accordion playing a soft, nostalgic song in one of the many alleyways of the district. He followed the sound as he departed from the cobbled street into a small alleyway that led up the hill. There before him in a window, sat a nude prostitute whose stare was as hypnotic as that of Victorine Meurent's in Edouard Manet's 'Olympia.' As he walked nearer to her, she did not remove her eyes from him. He felt his own invisible desires drawing him closer to her.

"Mademoiselle," he said, "I am a stranger in your city. I cannot speak French."

"Englishman, I can speak your language. What do you seek that I might offer you as a gift?"

William responded, "Your command of English is apparent. I seek the pleasure of your company. What is your name?"

"Céline," she replied.

"May I come in?" William asked politely, removing his hat to reveal the thickness of his black hair.

"Not here. You must wait outside until I am ready. Then you can take me to the Cabaret Le Bal du Montmartre."

"I am not familiar with the cabaret: perhaps somewhere else?"

"No, Englishman, it must be the Cabaret Le Bal du Montmartre."

"Please, Céline, call me 'William.'"

He stood outside in the warm Paris evening waiting for her. Soon she appeared fashionably dressed in a pale green gown embroidered in white silk.

"I am truly amazed by your beauty," William said as he gazed upon her.

William could not help but stare at her dark eyes and tightly woven hair; her shape further augmented by the corset she wore. He felt as though a dream had materialized before him; unsure, unsafe yet he was drawn to her.

Each evening he would arrive at her doorstep. She never asked him to enter her chamber, but instead would immediately close the door and lead him, arm in arm, to the Cabaret Le Bal du Montmartre.

She knew other women in the cabaret that spoke fluid French to their acquaintances; soulless women with eyes that wandered over his body as though considering the purchase of a commodity. The barman was a large man of Irish descent who had ventured into Paris as a young man and had soon found himself unable to leave the allurements he had found there. His graying red hair was thinning; his eyes beginning to sag with age. As he talked, he managed to keep a cigarette between his lips that bounced to the fluidity of his words,.

William asked, "Céline, why does the barman never speak to anyone except when required by his profession and then only in French?"

"Some say he killed a man in Dublin when he was young. The man he killed was an English army officer; the barman was a young freedom fighter. That is why he fled to the mainland. It was later told by a barmaid at the Moulin Rouge that he became a priest in Belgium; then after he was defrocked, he moved to Paris."

"Why was he defrocked? Did he kill again?" asked William.

"No, he had not taken the life of another. He was found with a woman in the confessional of the church," she replied.

"The only confessionals I have known are too small for two people to be in simultaneously; even if both are kneeling." William laughed.

"They were remodeling the church at the time and the bishop had secured the loan of a small portable compartment."

"I see," replied William. Occasionally the barman would stare at William with eyes that depicted both suspicion and obvious displeasure.

Many evenings were spent in the Cabaret Le Bal du Montmartre; a smoke-filled bar less famous for its noted clientele than for the absinthe it served to the melancholy crowd who appeared as a congregation seeking resolution for their sins. The yellow drink poured over a sugarcube soon took possession of both the mind and the body of the misbegotten. William realized that he, too was becoming a bond servant to both Céline and the drink.

The bars of Montmartre never closed. Eventually the clientele, however, must retreat to their apartments, hotels and barges along the Seine. Before the sun's appearance, in the earliest of twilight moments, Céline and William would walk back to a small hotel room on the street level. There they would talk about literature until they both collapsed into a deep sleep. Their affair was not that of the body, but of the mind.

Being a frequent visitor to Shakespeare and Company, Céline had a considerable knowledge of English and American authors; the small bookstore close to the banks of the Seine. In addition, she often visited various art exhibitions within the city; a mutual love that drew them both together. "How odd," he thought, "that I would find such a beautiful mind in the alleyways of Montmartre."

When alone and free of drink, William would, however, ask himself, "What insanity has possessed me?" He knew the rejection of Maud Gonne had destroyed his ego and cast him into depression from which he might not escape. He realized that Céline DuBois was but a temporary relief to his feelings of loss; a temporary fulfillment of the desire that loneliness had created.

In the evenings, Céline and William frequently walked together along the Seine, watching the barges pass by on the river; like his brother Jack, he was fascinated about capturing movement whether in words or in art. The changing colors of the light upon the bridges riveted his attention as though each bridge was painted anew upon their arrival.

Céline had been a dancer when she very young. She told William that had her mother not died so early, she would have trained to become a ballerina. Céline said her mother was from a well-bred aristocratic family; William knew better. The truth was by far a more interesting story yet held in low esteem and was not to be told.

On their walks, Céline would burst into an impromptu dance fashioned by music from a nearby cabaret. Her body in motion provided a variety of swirling colors like that of a kaleidoscope.

Fall had come to Paris and with it the cold rain and incessant cloud cover yet there were moments when the clouds would flee as though pierced by the Eiffel Tower. It was on such an evening that they walked together discussing the various histories of the cabarets and restaurants of Paris.

As they strolled enjoying the lingering warm air of the day, Céline began to dance. As she moved to the rhythm of the music, her heel caught fast in the trolley track. Suddenly she fell backwards as she called to William, "Forgive me!"

He heard her body strike the surface of the cold water. As he peered, her body disappeared into the murky, rapidly, flowing Seine.

He quickly dropped his topcoat and dove into the frigid water. In panic, he could not locate her. "Céline, Céline!" he called.

He swam to where he thought she had vanished and dove into the silt-laden, murky water that flowed swiftly to the Atlantic.

He swam violently back and forth, stopping only to shout her name. Finally exhausted, he clung to a lifebuoy that had been cast from a passing barge that stopped in the water ahead of him.

The crew pulled him from the murky water and covered him with a warm blanket. They were largely Brits that had been employed by a grain company to carry freight down the Seine to waiting ships.

"I am sorry, sir," a crewman said as he handed William a cup of warm rum. "You did all you could. There is too much current; I doubt her body will ever be found."

The crew then let him off alongside the quay of the river. "Sir, please keep the blanket." A most kind offer since he begun to shiver in the early night air.

That night, he sat alone in the hotel room. There was no solace for him as he wept. He asked himself a question that he could not answer: Can I love and be loved in return?

From the day of her death, he often wondered what she meant by the words "Forgive me."

The rain continued to fall in sheets of moisture outside the shop as Mary spoke softly. "Sir, do you think the spirit of Céline is following you?"

"No, I do not think she would wish me harm. I tried to save her life. If there had been more time, I believe we would have been lovers."

"Shall I ask the board another question?" she asked.

They placed their hands upon the board again. "Spirit who walks this night. Name yourself!"

Suddenly the planchette began to race across the board. Mary applied force to return it to its original position. "Spirit who walks the night! Name yourself!"

The planchette once more shot across the room hitting William in the chest. Stunned, he reacted to the pain that now throbbed within him.

"Sir, we must stop the session! I do not know what is happening but something evil walks the night. If you fear for your life, you may sleep in this room until the light returns to the streets. I will lock all of the doors. They are of heavy wood. Nothing can enter into this room except through the passage that leads from my bedroom."

"You are most kind, Mary. I will accept your invitation for I am very tired and do not wish to reenter a night filled with such apprehension and fear."

"Very well, sir. I will get you some blankets."

Mary returned with two large, wool blankets and laid them upon the fireside stool.

William listened to the voices of the night; the sounds of rain and cracking hearth. Soon he was experiencing fitful dreams in which a woman without a face, covered by a heavy black cape, pursued him throughout Saint Stephen's Green. When he stopped to rest, she would stop also; a faceless stare upon him.

He awoke thinking, "What hell have I been cast into? In my pursuit of being loved, I have truly brought no harm to anyone intentionally. Who pursues me and to what intent?"

When he left the shop at the break of light, he heard nothing from the bedchamber of Mary. It was as though she had vanished with the darkness. When he reentered the street, he noticed that her display window had been changed from the night before. Instead of the Ouija board and tarot cards, red roses in a crystal vase had been placed in their former position on a red cloth.

He returned to Saint Stephen's Green and sat on a bench as the sun arose behind the black clouds of a Dublin morning. Seagulls called to one another. Those who had slept under newspapers and old woolen blankets the night before were now quickly vanishing into the alleyways.

The odors of peat fires and the smells of bakery goods drifted in the wind. As he sat there, he thought again about Maud Gonne and her unimaginable beauty; a beauty that haunted him as truly as did the vision of the Woman of the Mist; each unobtainable as though both good and evil were seen but remained beyond his reach. Maud Gonne, now more than ever, haunted his thoughts in the dawn light of the Dublin morning when cold winter wind blew from off the Wicklow Mountains and down into the valleys on its journey to the Irish Sea.

❧ 30 ❧
Maud Gonne

Ever since he had met Maud at his father's art studio, he had known that he loved her. Even though he considered himself at least average in appearance, her beauty made him feel a court jester before her. How could anyone of such beauty ever love the plainness of so common a man?

"Perhaps," he reasoned, "my words, yes, my words, can convince her to love me."

From his love for her were to come forth poems, plays and essays. She had unwittingly released the creativity he had never known before. His writings were to bring forth the fictitious manners of the heart before the world's stage.

"When I arrive in Paris again, she will have had an opportunity to have read my works," he reasoned. "She is a lover of literature and will surely have read about me in some of the literary papers. I must however, be successful, yes, even great, for her to think of me. I shall prove myself worthy of her love."

Maud had early ignored the aspiring poet except for the flirtations of her youth; a light touch, a lingering stare. Later, she was to seek men whose convictions were not confined to words alone, but who translated their lives into action; such men like Lucien Millevoye and John McBride. They were everything she was looking for; men who were willing to give their lives for a cause. She, like Lady Gregory, was consumed in her passion for the nationalistic cause of Irish freedom.

After ringing the bell next to the red wooden double doors of the address where he believed Maud Gonne lived, he waited impatiently for a member of the household staff to arrive. He had sent a wire earlier in the week announcing his intended arrival. He did not know whether he would be greeted by her child, a husband or a lover; such were the uncertainties of their relationship.

Soon the doors opened. "Good morning, I am William. Is Madame Gonne at home?" he asked standing on the stone steps that led to her apartment.

"Please follow me, sir. Madame Gonne has been expecting you." As they walked, he looked out onto a garden in which a fountain splashed its waters upon brilliant yellow, red and orange flowers where butterflies rested. He even thought for a moment that he spotted a Beautiful Demoiselle dragonfly, native to southern Ireland, with its luminescent greens.

William was pleasantly surprised at the Victorian appearance of her apartment and garden. Inside, tall ceilings and light green walls highlighted the various works of local artists. A fine oak bookcase held many leather-bound volumes of literature with their gold-leafed wording.

Maud was seated in a fireside chair as he entered the room. She arose, and then lightly kissed him on both cheeks before being seated again; the warmth of her hands sliding from his own.

"William, I am pleased you have decided to visit me again while you are staying in Paris. Is it work or pleasure that has brought you this time to our city? Some say it is more beautiful than Dublin. I, however, will not agree with them. Cities are but stone and wood. It is within the hearts of people that I find the greatest expression of beauty."

He did not know whether to tell her the truth; that he had returned to Paris to see only her. He did not care about the buildings or the many monuments that lined the boulevards. Had she dwelt in a fisherman's stone house on the Connemara coast, he would have come to her. He felt that his life had no meaning without her. Within himself, he acknowledged his vulnerability to this most fair of women.

"Maud, I understand your love for the Irish cause, but does it allow room for others to love you and for you to love them in return?"

"William, you have asked a question that betrays your thoughts."

"Maud, your perception has always been keener than my words. I cannot hide my true feelings from you."

"Well spoken, William. Then rephrase your intent."

"As you know, I have always desired to be near you, yet you refuse my quest."

"How silly of you to think of love as a quest,' she responded. "It must be spontaneous; not ordained or rehearsed. There are no formulas to be applied to the relationship between a man and a woman. If I am attracted to the whole of a person; then love will come naturally. If not, the suitor is pursuing the impossible."

"Where have I fallen so short in my desire for you?"

"I cannot force love that does not exist. I admire you too much to be dishonest with you. You have scorned my religious faith and my strong sense of devotion to the Irish people."

She gently took his hand; resting it lightly within her own. "William, we are more than just two people. You look upon me as a man would who wades in the shallow waters of a tropical sea; you see only beauty and nothing more. You have not looked deep into my soul nor sought to know more of me than how I look, or what I am wearing.

Do you not understand? I am more than a physical object for you to admire and then grow old with. What happens when I am old and the beauty of youth has faded? Could you love me then?"

"Maud, as you know, I cannot have you anymore than your desire for me allows. I can neither advance nor retreat in my love for you. You dwell in the words I write on the pages in my study. You possess me both night and day; awake and in my dreams. I would that my heart could flee from you, but it cannot."

"William, I am twenty-two and you are but twenty-three. We have our lives before us. Do not ask me to settle for less; let my dreams continue to be free, for without them, I will perish inside and what you love will die."

"Maud, is there no respite for me? Where can I turn to that you will not be present? On the Irish Sea, you are there; in the Wicklow Mountains, I hear your voice. My soul cannot escape your presence. I am but the rich man calling out from hell."

"You see me not as I am. Then let me dwell upon your pages. Create me as you will."

William felt as though he were drowning. He could not reach the surface from where he had plunged. Yes, he had expressed his affection for others, but that was of little comfort. Like the sun hidden behind the cloudy drapes of an Irish Day, the clarity of his thoughts had vanished. He did not know how to pursue her, yet he knew she could be won by others.

William had earlier let her know that he could not bring himself to accept the tenets of her Catholic faith nor her extreme passion for the cause of the landless poor. Instead he wanted their love to be sublime like words written in a poem; a directed force of expression.

He then uttered words he knew were impossible for him to believe, "Let us meet then within a verse; words written upon a page; a love without an embrace."

The sounds of the gulls and the splashing of the park's fountain created a new image from the past; a woman he had too soon forgotten.

❧ 31 ❧

Countess Markievicz

His thoughts took him to Constance Georgine Gore-Booth, later to become Countess Georgine Markievicz, whom he had grown to adore as a child while visiting Lissadell Houe, her country estate in County Silgo. Lissadell House was a symbol of wealth and prestige; a state of mind unobtainable except to those born in the aristocratic class of the landed gentry. Constance soon became a beautiful young girl with long legs and well-defined features. Later they were to share a mutual friend, Maud Gonne.

Constance in her youth came under the spell of the young, aspiring writer. His world was one of words. She, like Maud, was to later become consumed by the need to reform the political and social environments of Ireland. In youth, however, a poet's words held command over her emotions.

William remembered their last meeting at Lissadell House. "Constance, you are indeed a most beautiful and charming hostess," said William. He greatly admired her ability to capture emotions in oils. "Your ability to paint landscapes surpasses even that of my brother's," he said with a smile.

"William, I cannot confess to such a talent. Jack is by far the superior artist. My sole talent lies in my ability to convey emotions as only a woman can. I think emotions rule my sex as violence does yours."

"I hope not all men are as narrowly focused as that," William replied. "Constance, you are not limited by your sex. Instead it frees you to explore your creative talent in ways no man can."

"William, since childhood we have been friends. I only wish it could have been more, but you were never interested enough in me to pursue more than my friendship. Perhaps neither my appearance nor my intellect was sufficient enough for you."

"Constance, I was always in awe of your beauty and the strengths that radiated from you even as a child. How can a man love a person who is far superior to himself?"

"William, as is your nature, you select words that flatter."

"I have never hidden from your presence," answered William. "Let us walk down to the sea and look upon the waves that too soon will alter the beaches of County Sligo. They are larger than usual."

They walked to the stone-strewn beach. Arm in arm they strolled not as lovers but as friends. Once on the sand, they removed their shoes and waded into the distant gulf-warmed waters. Petrels and gulls screamed for attention above the crashing waves. Suddenly they stopped walking and looked into each other's eyes.

"Constance, I was foolish not to pursue you. I know you will move to Paris soon in order to enroll in the Academie Julian. I know it is difficult for a woman in Dublin to aspire to be an artist. I feel that you will meet someone who soon will become your lover. Our time together is now too short. In youth, we played together and created imaginary places where time did not exist. I know I should have returned home to Sligo and to Lissadell House.

We could have become such good friends; perhaps even lovers. We are very similar, you and I."

He laced his hands about her waist and drew her next to him. With an embrace, he kissed her with a passion unknown to him, and then released her.

Once more the sound of the fountain in Saint Stephen's Green returned him to the present and to the emptiness within his heart.

❧ 32 ❧

Glendalough

The day was cooler than he expected as he boarded the Dublin bus for the short trip to the Wicklows; those small mountains that lie so close to Dublin yet ignored by most of the city's residence; their forest and meadows of multiple colors of green.

Lady Gregory had arrived by car; a long black car that could not help but be noticed by the elite tourist population of Glendalough; a statement made; some might say a shout of opulence in a time of uncertainty. She had received his invitation to see her only a day before. He knew she would be in Dublin arranging or at least trying to arrange a physical location for their hoped-for theater. He had expected his invitation to be rejected.

Glendalough was as much a location of the imagination as that of reality. An early monastic settlement; its appeal growing on tourists yet still too remote for the poor of Dublin to venture forth; a place of holy contemplation among the mountain streams and virgin forest of the Wicklow Mountains. A place of stone buildings serrated by the wind and rains of centuries.

It was to him as beautiful up close as it was from a distance; the precision of the monastic stonework was truly amazing. Flowing water was abundantly present as were meadow flowers that sought the light within the rim of the forest meadows.

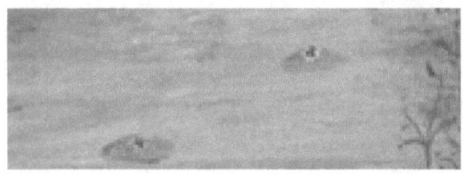

Two lakes; two dreams of what life should be. William had decided once more to confront her regarding his affections; desires unfulfilled; bare of a rational understanding. They met by the gate of the monastery; stone steps leading to the monastic buildings and cemetery filled with graves of long dead saints and sinners.

In the ninth century, St. Kevin had made his bed nearby in the cliffs above the lower lake. His lover, after his rejection of her, had fallen from his den that was hewn from the face of a sheer stone cliff above the lake. As she fell for only a moment, he looked upon her red hair as she descended into the frigid waters of the lake below. He, like

Augusta, had decided that his life was of a singular pursuit without time for the love of another. History does not regard the loneliness and tears that followed.

Augusta looked only briefly at William as they walked up the lower steps to enter the settlement of stone buildings and Celtic crosses. Their feet treading upon stones and wet earth; crows calling from the nearby fields of ancient cedars that lined the walkways around the sides of the two lakes.

They did not speak until the light was hidden by the overhanging branches of the dark, green cedars. The sounds of running water and forest birds accompanied them.

"Augusta, we have known each other for many years yet we remain together and apart. Why have we chosen to exist as both lovers and strangers?" he asked.

"Even in our youth, we discussed this," she replied. "I know you never really accepted the answers I gave to you."

"They were but hollow answers," said William. "Love is not a difficult thing to understand. It is the most elementary of feelings. It is the natural fulfillment of our urges both physically and emotionally. In and of itself, it does not have to be consumed like one shares a bottle of wine. I have never withheld my emotions from you, yet I feel they were not returned."

"You are foolish to think they were not given. What could I have given more than my body and my thoughts to you? Nothing was held back," said Augusta. "To be sanctioned by another whether they be holy or foul means nothing to me."

"Why was our love not made known to the world?" said William. "I know the reasons you have continued to give me. Have you not outwardly rejected me yet burned within as I have?"

"I could not yield to the possession of both my mind and body to another no matter how great a poet you had become. It would have destroyed us both," she replied.

They walked past a small waterfall. "Listen, the sounds of the water both comfort and invite me. If only time could remain as this waterfall has since the time of St. Kevin. It is the earth's eternal voice," said Augusta.

"How foolish for time is not ours to hold onto. We are no more eternal than the birds that fly over this lake. The falcon we see today is not the one that sings tomorrow. Time is our own illusion," said William.

"Tell me, would you have loved me as a friend or as a possession had we married?" asked Augusta.

"You speak more as a riddler from the alleyways on Grafton Street. What is possession but the longing to be near? Can one be near and not touch? What is there to be fearful of? I offered but the most gentle of love," said William.

Augusta knelt to feel the cold water that collected below the natural fountain. She then moistened a cloth and pressed it to her forehead as though anointing herself with previous oils.

"Why," asked William, "do you place the tumbled waters of the mountain stream on your forehead for the day is cool? Are you to adorn yourself with the waters of this mountain?"

"To touch that which has flowed from the bosom of the earth gives but meaning to it." She then cupped her hands and drank from the waters of the pool that reflected the green forest leaves and whose bottom was cobbled by small stones of different colors and shapes. "You see, I am now part of that which is eternal. I drank from the fountain though it is not owned nor possessed by me. Am I now wed to these waters though a priest has not blessed it with the sacraments of the church? I am blessed without possession; free to drink and thirst."

She rose and faced him. Her eyes filled with warmth that he had not seen since Coole Park. Her eyes invited him as the air invites the falcon to fly. He hesitated a moment, transfixed by her eyes. To yield to her physical desire was to admit defeat, to bestow victory to her that could not be redeemed.

He moved towards her, hesitant at first; then reached for her as the prodigal son did the embrace of his father. They touched as young lovers do when they have rediscovered their love in the morning sun; the time between the dream and the remainder of the day.

~33~
The Abbey Theater

The new century had arrived and with it, a growing sense of the role that Ireland was to play in the world of literature and the performing arts. The dreams of Lady Gregory, Edward Martyn and William had been realized in the first performance at the Abbey Theater. There was nothing to stop them now and their shared dream of an Irish literary revival. Augusta had formed her life's works upon Aristotle's "Express yourself like the common people, but think like a wise man."

That evening Augusta and William arrived early and seated themselves in a private gallery. They wanted to observe the faces of the patrons as they watched the performance of their new play.

"Augusta, may I congratulate you on your vision," said William.

"Only if you share the congratulations," she responded with a smile.

"We should have married years ago. Your too lofty ideas prevented us from the greatest joys of life."

"I think you are wrong, William. We remained lovers and friends. How many married couples can still say that? I would have lost you had I given myself completely to you. I could not so gamble when the odds were apparent to me."

"Life is more than percentages," he replied smiling at her as the seated guests looked up admiringly at the two figures seated in a box above the ground floor of the theater.

"What amazes me so much, Augusta, is that there were never any rumors in the press or anywhere else about our love for one another," said William as he leaned towards her seat.

"It seems that many chose to look the other way for the sake of Ireland's literary movement. We all knew a scandal could have destroyed everything at the beginning," Augusta replied.

"Still I wonder what if we had taken a different path – a path together when we departed Thoor Ballylee that summer so long ago?" William questioned.

"I do not know how to judge what might have been. I only know this glorious night exists as does my love for you," she said while grasping his hand tightly.

Soon the lights dimmed and all eyes gazed upon the lighted stage as the curtain rose. At that moment, William looked into Augusta's eyes, pulled her close to him, and pursued his true feelings for her in a prolonged and passionate kiss; a kiss unseen by the audience whose attention was now drawn to the lighted stage.

"I love you," William said.

"And I you," she replied.

～34～
The Prophecy of Killarney

It was at the Fitzgerald Hotel in Dublin that he overheard two professors from Trinity College talking about a lady who had been diagnosed with breast cancer. From the tone of their conversation, she had been very famous in the early 20th Century.

William laid down his newspaper and turned towards the gentlemen. "Sirs, I could not help but hear you discussing a woman who had a profound impact on the Irish Literary Revival. Please tell me of whom you speak."

"Sir," responded one of the professors. "It is widely rumored that Lady Augusta Gregory of Coole Park is very ill. I understand from my wife that she heard Lady Gregory had been experiencing difficulties in breathing and had sought a medical opinion after she discovered a rather large lump in one of her breasts."

"Sir, you cannot be correct," responded William rather forcefully. "I know her ladyship and she is quite well. She would have let me know otherwise."

"Pardon me, sir, I meant no offense. I am just quoting my wife who has relatives in Gort. She is a sister of the doctor's wife who examined Lady Gregory. I am certain it has not been reported in any paper due to a respect for her privacy. By the way, do I know you?"

William did not respond but looked out the large plate-glass window into Saint Steven's Green where young children were chasing one another in the bright sunlight that had quickly followed an Irish shower. Despite his immediate rejection of the gentleman's comments regarding Lady Gregory, he sensed the truth of her condition.

He arose from the table and quickly left the Fitzgerald on his way to Kingsbridge Station. He hurriedly bought a ticket to Galway and a transfer to Gort.

The evening was late when he arrived at Coole Park. Already the sounds of early evening had entered into the glades.

He pounded loudly upon the door. Suddenly Mary opened the door. "Sir, we were not expecting you at Coole Park." William could see that Mary, that loyal servant of so many years, had been crying; her beautiful blue eyes now reddened by tears.

"Mary, is it true what I have heard?" he asked firmly holding both of her shoulders in his hands.

"Yes, sir, her Ladyship is very ill."

With those words, William embraced her; his tears moistening her hair. "Mary, Mary, what am I to do?" he pleaded.

"Sir, there is nothing you can do. Only the Virgin Mother can save her. Pray, sir, for her soul."

"Take me to her," William said quietly, having released her from his embrace.

"Yes, sir, she is seated in the library. I know she will be happy that you are here. May I take your coat and the portfolio case you are carrying?"

"Please do take my overcoat. I will keep the portfolio case with me," said William.

William entered the library. "Augusta, my beloved."

"I am here, William," she said quietly.

At first he could not see her in the darkening room for the sun was now hidden by the branches of the tall beech and oak trees. The ticking of the clock and the voice of the fire were the only sounds he heard as his eyes searched the room. There in a large leather chair sat Augusta; her shoulders wrapped in a red shawl; the one that he had given her years previously when they had met in Dublin. Her dress was a white linen material which highlighted the blue diamond about her neck. Her hair, having turned grayer, was the same texture he had loved as a young man when his fingers would weave through its many varied colors that changed with the light.

Her eyes seemed large and blue yet she appeared much smaller than he remembered. The disease was destroying her more quickly than he had imagined.

"My beloved Augusta." He hesitated and could not speak as he lowered himself to place his head upon her lap. She could feel the tears reaching her skin through the linen dress. She did not speak as she stroked his graying hair softly.

"My beloved William," she said. "Is it not what must be? Could we have asked for more than what has been given to us?"

"Augusta, the fairies are crueler that I could have ever thought. They commanded me to love you and yet we could not be as one. The waste! The waste of it all!" He laid his head upon her legs and wept loudly in the darkening, silent room.

He arose from his kneeling position. "My beloved, I have brought you a gift. It is a gift that you cannot open. It must remain as it is; hidden from all to view," said William.

"What gift can I receive, yet not see?" she asked. Augusta looked at the portfolio case William held in his right hand; the leather new and well oiled.

"My quest to know more about the spirit world took me to the wild fields and mountains of Killarney. I had heard from a villager that a woman with great gifts lived near a lake at the foot of the oxbow mountains. While dining at a local pub, I learned she had frequent contact with the fairies; perhaps she herself was their queen since her knowledge was so great. The strangers also told me that though she was centuries old, she would appear to me both young and beautiful; such were her powers to deceive.

"As I sauntered along the sweet-smelling trails bordered by heather, I discovered a most unusual dwelling. From what appeared as no more than an abandoned home of loosely piled stones, smoke was pouring from its chimney. At first, I thought it to be an ancient cairn like that of Queen Maeve's atop Knocknarea in County Sligo. The smell of peat and other herbs could be sensed as I entered the pathway to the home announcing my presents with a loud voice.

"The wooden door of the hut slowly opened. Before me stood a woman in her youth with long black hair and hazel eyes that reached into my soul.

"'My sir, you travel a path that only leads to the lakes and sea of Kildare. What do you seek? Love, knowledge, immortality?' she said.

"'To a writer, the three cannot be separated. They are joined as a trinity," I responded.

"'Then enter my dwelling,' she said with a deceptive smile. 'For a gold coin I will tell you what you seek.'

"I did not know how much money I had in my pockets, but I gave her everything that I possessed.

"The strange woman then said, 'If the trinity you spoke of is what you seek, then take something of the twain and place the reflection of you both in a secret place where it will not be found until you both be dead.'

"I told her about the paintings that had captured my feelings for you; the paintings I have never shown to you." Augusta remained silent as he continued to speak. "She told me to go to the well of Saint Bridget and there to follow the pagan stones until I reached the last remaining oak of the ancient Druid wood. When I questioned the significance of a Christian site, she reminded me that when the ice covered Sliabh Liag, it had been the sacred site of the gathering of the old ones and the source of the spring was a fairy well. She told me to take a strand of ivy from the great oak tree, the last remaining of the sacred grove of Kildare, and wrap the strand around the paintings in the form of a love knot woven from my lover's hair."

William continued, "She said that when the images are later to be discovered and revealed; as the knot is untied; the paintings will appear as though they had just been completed. The colors will be vibrant and if one listens, the wind and sounds of water will be heard. Birds will fly above the turloughs of Coole Park, and the one that opens it will hear the call of a raven. The image of lovers now reflected in oils will embrace once more. When the lovers embrace, they will be as they are in the work of art; to live forever in the Seven Woods of Coole."

William then handed the ivy-wrapped portfolio case to Augusta.

"William, I am impressed by your fanciful story. I should have asked you for input when I was collecting my stories related to early Irish folk tales. It doesn't hurt to believe in a child's story of immortality and love. I will place the portfolio in my secret hiding place. There it will remain until my death. I will instruct that it not be removed or opened until word of your death has reached Coole Park. Only then will its contents be revealed."

Later after William departed, Augusta said to Mary, "Place the portfolio behind the wall paneling in my secret place where it must remain untouched until both William and I are dead."

There the portfolio was to remain until the destruction of Coole House. When found by the destruction crew, the love knot of ivy was still wrapped around the portfolio of paintings.

The professor awoke as the flame died upon its own ashes. The last embers of the fire emitted a gray smoke that quickly vanished into the now darkened chimney as chill, uninvited, once more entered the room.

The hall clock sounded and Mt. Gilead was silent.

On September 26th 1998 this Sundial,
commissioned by Dúchas The Heritage Service
was unveiled by
Lady Gregory's granddaughters
'Me and Nu'.

.....our shadows rove the garden gravel still ...." (W.B

Ar an 26 ú Meán Fómhair 1998 nochtaíodh an Clog Gr
a choimisiúnaigh Dúchas An tSeirbhís Oidhreac
ag gariníonacha na Bantiarna Gregory,
'Me agus Nú'

".....siúlann ar scáthanna ar fán go fóill
ar fud ghairbhéal an ghairdín....." (W.B. Yeats

he Heritage Service

Within the gardens of Coole Park are the words:

.....our shadows rove the garden gravel still....

W.B. Yeats

About the Author

Franklin Lafayette King is the author of *The Woman in the Window*, *Sunflowers and Zinnias*, *Hauntings of a Summer Moon* and *The Poet Who Writes upon Water* — all published by Texture Press.